TRAPPED BY THE MAFIA BOSS

A FORCED MARRIAGE ITALIAN MAFIA ROMANCE

THE FORCED MARRIAGE MAFIA BOSSES
BOOK 2

MARIA FROST

SLOANE CAMERON PUBLISHING

Copyright © 2024 Maria Frost
Cover © 2024 - covers_by_wonderland

All rights reserved.

No part of this book may be reproduced in any form or by any electronic or mechanical means, including information storage and retrieval systems, without written permission from the author.

TRIGGER WARNINGS

Trapped by the Mafia Boss contain the following tropes and potential triggers:

Tropes:

- Protective and obsessed billionaire mafia boss hero
- Instalove
- Age gap, she's 19, he's 40
- Kidnapping
- Forced marriage
- Virgin heroine
- Spanking/sub-dom elements

Potential Triggers:

- Cursing
- Sex on the page (masturbation, spanking, dirty talk, anal)
- Violence on the page including interrogation

- Death of minor characters
- Domestic violence in childhood (backstory)

BLURB

I had a steamy encounter with a mafia boss twice my age. Big mistake.

When I was a child, my parents called me useless.

But now I'm a struggling playwright desperately trying to get my life together.

Until the day my elevator breaks down and I'm trapped with a silver fox mafia boss.

Cue the return of my panic attacks and I can't breathe anymore.

He doesn't just calm me down, he makes me fall hard for his soothing voice.

Before I know it, my fear has vanished along with all my clothes.

But when the doors suddenly open all hell breaks loose.

Because his enemies want him dead and now I'm a witness to their brutal attack.

There's only one way I can survive.

I have to leave behind everything I know and marry the obsessive mobster.

I've sacrificed a lot in my life to get where I am.

But I never thought that one day I'd have to sacrifice my heart to a killer in an Italian suit.

1

ISABELLA

I'm waiting for the elevator when an Italian God appears next to me. "Going down?" he asks, reaching past to hit the elevator call button.

I wipe my eyes, managing to mumble, "Uh, yeah."

God, he looks so good. Why did he have to catch me when I've only just stopped crying. I bet I look awful right now.

He's twice my age and drop-dead gorgeous. Silver threads blend into his tousled dark hair. He's wearing an impeccably tailored Italian suit that hugs his frame in all the right places.

I'm a mess. It's that simple.

Our eyes meet as I take another glance. A jolt of electricity arcs between us. It's as if he sees straight into the depths of my soul, seeing the fantasies I'm trying to hide from him.

Does he know how much I want him to take my virginity right now? That's the problem with being a playwright. You can't stop inventing scenarios in your head. Mine right now are rated X for extremely unlikely to happen.

The elevator dings, snapping me back to reality as the doors slide open.

"Isabella, right?" His voice is deep, a smooth caramel sound that makes my panties melt. "After you."

I step into the elevator, frowning as he joins me. He never joins me. He just stands beside me until I enter the elevator, and then he walks away. Every time that's what happens.

What's different about today?

"How do you know my name?" I ask as the doors close in front of us.

His eyebrows quirk upwards as if he's not used to being questioned. "I know everything that happens in my building."

"Your building? The Caruso Building belongs to you? Are you...?"

"Dominic Caruso. A pleasure." He holds a hand out toward me. "You've been crying. Who hurt you? Say the name, and he's dead."

I manage a smile. "Just a rough writing workshop today. This guy was trying to flirt with me. Got pissy when I turned him down."

"You want me to kill him for you?"

I laugh, but his expression remains deadly serious. "I think we can let him live," I say eventually.

"Let me know if you change your mind. Screenwriting workshop, right?"

"Yeah but I'm writing a play. Anyway, a bunch of us get together to discuss our work once a week. Screenwriters, playwrights, we even have a couple of novelists.

"Anyway, this new guy joined this week, and he kept staring at me. Then he asked for my number and when I said no, he said I shouldn't turn down dates. Said I couldn't get offered many weighing as much as I do. Called me a fat pig when I turned him down."

His face turns dark. "You catch his name?"

There's a strange grinding sound. The elevator jolts violently, and then stops dead.

My heart leaps into my throat. "What just happened?"

"We appear to be stuck," he says, pressing the emergency button. He doesn't sound surprised. "Isn't this interesting? No one's answering. Been disconnected, it seems."

Panic claws at me. "Stuck? As in trapped? This is your building. Don't you handle the maintenance?"

He moves closer, his voice soothing. "Hey, it's okay. We'll be moving soon enough."

I try to breathe, but the air feels thick. "I'll message my people," he says, tapping on his cellphone.

The minutes tick by, the temperature increasing until I'm sweating like mad.

I pace up and down, my breathing becoming labored as Dominic continues to tap on his cellphone.

He looks up, noticing my discomfort. "You can take a layer or two off. Cool down a little."

"I'm all right, thanks."

"Don't worry, I won't tell anyone what I saw."

"I'm not getting my tits out in an elevator," I snap. "It'll be fixed quickly, right?"

"I've sent a message to my people, but there's no service. Have to see if it gets through."

"God, I hope it does. I can't breathe in here. It's too hot. Are you hot? I'm boiling."

"So take something off."

"I told you, I'm not getting undressed in an elevator, no matter how hot it gets."

"You'll feel better. Look, I'll go first." He starts unbuttoning his shirt, revealing a chiseled six-pack covered in tattoos and scars. I hold in a moan of desire but only just. Fuck, he looks so good, I can't help but stare.

"You're just going to strip like we're on a beach somewhere?"

He shrugs as a bead of sweat runs down his rippling abs. "It's hot, and we may be here a while." He folds his shirt and jacket, setting them down in the corner behind him. "Your turn. You'll feel better. Trust me."

"I can't," I mutter, but the fight is fading from my voice.

"You can and will," he orders, his voice becoming firmer. "Take off that jacket and undo your blouse now before you pass out."

"No."

He closes the space between us. "Fine, I'll just wait until you faint and then strip you anyway."

"You ever heard of consent, bud?"

"You heard of heat stroke? Remember, what happens in the elevator stays in the elevator. And for what it's worth, I happen to like those curves of yours. Wouldn't mind seeing some more of them."

Another couple of minutes pass and I feel myself getting woozy. "Stop being stubborn," he growls. "You'll hurt your head if you pass out."

"Oh, God," I mutter. "Fine, but I'm only taking off my jacket." I shrug it off my shoulders, muttering to myself. "I can't believe I'm doing this."

At once, I feel better. I loosen the top two buttons of my blouse, wafting the fabric with my hand.

The air is still stifling, but his approving smile eases my nerves. "Good girl," he says, taking my jacket from me. My panties, already melted, disappear forever. Praise, from him? Oh, God, take me already.

He nods my way. "Take that blouse off too. That's an order, Isabella."

I want to disobey him but I can't do it, not after he called me a good girl. My blouse is off an instant later, leaving me in my bra.

Despite the heat, my nipples harden under his hungry gaze. Can he see them through the lace? Can he see the effect his naked chest is having on me.

I picture him sweeping me into those arms of his, ripping my panties from my body before pushing me to the floor, telling me this is happening whether I want it to or not. Then thrusting his enormous...

"You okay?" he asks. "Looking a little flushed to me."

"Got any water?" I ask, hoping to splash it onto my face, though I think it might turn straight into steam.

"Afraid not."

"You know, I never guessed I'd spend my morning topless with the owner of the building."

"You're not topless. Not yet, anyway." He takes a step toward me. "Take off your bra. Let me see those rock hard nipples of yours. I know you want to, Isabella. Stop fighting your desire."

I want to pinch myself. He can't be saying that, can he? It must be a dream. I can't really be here with the man I'm obsessed with, hearing him tell me to take my bra off.

"Is that your chat up technique?" I ask. "Bit full on, isn't it?"

He doesn't smile. "Nice attempt at distraction. I've seen the way your pupils dilate whenever you see me. I've heard your breathing change when I stand next to you. I know you want me. Like I said, what happens in the elevator, stays in the elevator."

I shake my head. "Take off your pants first." I'm teasing him, but he accepts my challenge at once. "I didn't mean it," I add, but he's already slipping them off.

"There," he says with a flicker of a smile as I try not to look at his tight boxer shorts. "Like being on the beach back at

Portofino. Except without the sunshine. Or the sea. Or a decent drink."

"Portofino? Where's that?"

"Italy. Tiny little fishing village. It's where I was born. Now, are you removing that bra or am I?"

I glance down. There's a definite bulge growing in his boxer shorts.

I feel a corresponding throb between my legs. An emptiness that wasn't there before.

I want to reach out and grab that bulge. It's filled more of my dreams than I want anyone to know about.

"You know," he says, taking a step toward me. "We could fuck in here and no one would ever know."

"I've been in this building once a week for the last three months. Every time, I've bumped into you in the line for the elevators, you never say a word. "Now, you're saying that to me?"

"Only because I see you looking down at my cock. I see how hard your nipples are. You want me to fuck you. Am I wrong?"

I want him to take my V-card more than anything in the world. Just grab hold of me and take the decision out of my hands.

"What are you thinking right now?" he asks, lifting my chin with his finger. "Be honest."

I blurt out without thinking. "That if this crashes and we both die, I go out still a virgin."

Dominic raises an eyebrow. "That can soon be fixed."

"It's just an observation," I quip, but my heart races at the thought. I hope he doesn't make me take my pants off. My panties are soaked from the sight of that hard bulge in his boxer shorts.

The tension between us crackles, the heat turning from discomfort to desire. "My offer stands," he murmurs, closing the gap between us. "Wouldn't want you to die unfulfilled."

His breath is warm on my face, the electric current of his proximity sending shivers down my spine.

The confined space of the elevator feels even smaller as his muscled frame presses against mine. His scarred skin brushes against my bare arm, igniting a fire within me.

Without warning, he leans in closer, his lips grazing my earlobe. "I've been watching you," he whispers. "Watching those curves of yours. Been wanting to fuck you since the first time I saw you."

2

ISABELLA

He reaches for the waistband of his boxer shorts. In one swift motion, he pulls them down, stepping out of them and kicking them to the side. He takes hold of his huge cock, gripping the throbbing shaft.

"This is what you do to me," he says. "Every time I see that curvy ass of yours, those perfect tits, I get hard as fucking rock. You make it impossible to think of anything but fucking you. I'm obsessed with you, Isabella."

I stare at his cock, unable to take my eyes off it as he strokes himself slowly. "It hurts to look at you and not take you," he continues. "I've resisted for too long. I can't resist you any longer."

He leans closer, his lips an inch from mine. He grabs hold of me, pressing his naked body against mine.

He kisses me like we've been lovers for years, our tongues dancing in sync as the intensity of the moment washes over me.

I melt into his arms, my entire body going limp.

He breaks away from our kiss too soon, his gaze locked with mine as he slowly trails his fingers down my arm.

His touch sparks electricity along my skin, igniting a fire that courses through every fiber of my being. With practiced hands, he unhooks the clasp of my bra, letting it tumble silently to the ground.

He cups my buttocks, pulling me into his manly grip, his body pressed against mine. His cock touches me, hard and hot. He kisses me again. "My world, it's a dark place. I told myself to stay away, protect you from it. Keep you pure."

"What happens in the elevator stays in the elevator, right?"

My hands find their way to his chest, feeling the hard planes of his body beneath my fingers.

As he kisses me again, his fingers tug at the waistband of my pants, pulling them down my legs until they join the growing pile of clothing on the floor.

I can't help but gasp as his hands make their way into my panties, gently parting the folds of my most intimate place. "No one's ever touched me there," I whisper.

He pushes me back against the cold metal wall. Our bodies are still joined together in the intense heat of our passion. A finger slides inside me as I moan into his mouth.

"That feels so good," I tell him as he stares into my eyes.

He pulls the finger out, licking it slowly. "As sweet as I thought it would be," he says before leaning down, flicking his tongue over my aching nipples.

His fingers continue to tease me, his touch feather-light as he gently strokes my clit, causing my body to tremble with pleasure.

He looks up at me, his eyes burning with desire as he reads my mind. He smiles, his eyes never leaving mine as he grabs a condom from his wallet. He slips it on before positioning himself between my legs

Every muscle in his body ripples with anticipation, yet he remains calm and self-assured. "Trust me," he says. "Take deep breaths."

Just before he enters me, he pauses, his eyes locked onto mine. A gentle, reassuring smile crosses his face as he whispers, "Breathe with me."

I feel the warmth of his breath on my ear, and I obey, taking slow and deep breaths with him. The rhythm of our breathing synchronizes, and for a moment, I forget about my nerves.

His body trembles with restraint, every fiber of his being focused on making sure I am comfortable and safe. And I am - in his presence, I feel completely at ease.

His hands grip my hips, holding me steady as he eases into me. I wince and he pauses, checking I'm okay. I manage a smile. "I'm not made of china," I say, reaching up and kissing him. "Don't worry."

His cock grows bigger within me, and I can't help but want more. "Deeper," I whisper as he rocks back and forth, my voice becoming hoarse with desire.

He needs no further encouragement, moving further into me, stretching my pussy, filling me with his length. The sensation is so intense it tips me toward the edge of a climax.

"Come for me," he commands. His voice is demanding, and I feel fear and desire wash over me. "Do you want me?" he adds, his words dripping with authority.

"So much."

"Show me. Come for me. Come around my cock." He grips my ass, lifting me into the air, lowering me onto his shaft, impaling me on his length.

I want to resist, to deny him the satisfaction of my surrender. But my body betrays me, responding to his command with an overwhelming need for him.

I slip a hand between us, easing the ache in my clit. I rub it frantically as he thrusts faster.

My entire being quivers and shakes under his touch, a primal need to surrender to the intense pleasure coursing through my veins.

A tidal wave of ecstasy builds within me, crashing over me with unstoppable force. Every inch of my body trembles and convulses in pure pleasure as my orgasm hits more powerfully than any I've ever given myself.

With a final thrust, he releases inside of me, filling me with a warm, pulsing energy that leaves my body tingling in its wake. He grunts as it happens, his fingers digging into my ass, holding me tightly against him.

The elevator jerks to life and I'm instantly panicking. He slides out of me, lowering me to my feet. I grab hold of my clothes and climb into them, fearing the doors opening before I'm ready.

"Oh shit," I mutter, fumbling to do up the buttons of my blouse.

Dominic does it for me, his face a picture of calm. By the time the doors open, it looks like nothing happened. Except for my red face, messed up hair, and the dull ache between my legs where he took my V-card.

I'm no longer a virgin. The man I dream about every night was my first. I can't help but grin. As long as I don't wake up, this is going to be a day I remember for a very long time.

I step out in a daze, not noticing I'm alone.

"This isn't the lobby," he says, glancing past me. "Someone set me up. Rewired the buttons."

"Why? Who would do that?"

"Get back inside," he adds, stepping in front of me. "Now."

"The door's already closed."

He hammers the elevator call button, still staring down the corridor. "Clever boys," he mutters.

My breath hitches as I glance past him. Six men are standing about twenty yards away, ski masks concealing their identities, guns ominously pointed in our direction.

The elevator dings open. With lightning reflexes, Dominic thrusts me inside, vaulting in behind me.

The doors slide shut too sluggishly, and an armed intruder sprints forward, wedging an arm through the narrowing gap.

In a blur of movement, Dominic seizes the arm, snapping it with a sickening crack. He shoves the assailant with such force that the man stumbles backward, flung as if weightless.

Yet, the odds are tipping against us. He parries gun after gun getting in through the gap, but the inevitability of a bullet finding its mark looms over me like a dark cloud. Desperation claws at my throat.

In a frantic bid for safety, my fingers dance over the elevator panel, slamming every button in a chaotic plea for closure.

The doors inch together as yet another assailant lunges at us with gun primed.

"Down!" I scream, tugging Dominic away from the line of fire. The pistol fires, the noise making my ears ring.

In a final act of defiant protection, Dominic kicks out, sending the attacker reeling back so the elevator doors can close, cutting us off from the chaos outside.

I'm left gasping as we descend, my heart racing. Dominic stands up, examining the hole in the wall where the bullet hit.

"You saved my life," he says in an amused voice.

"Who were they?" I ask, my voice barely above a whisper.

He looks down at me, and fear courses through my veins. He no longer looks like a man. He looks like the devil and I cower before that glare.

"They're dead men."

3

DOMINIC

"Why did you want to meet me here?" Jerry asks, picking up a book of nude paintings from the shelf beside him. "Since when do we frequent bookshops?"

I snatch the book from him and return it to the shelf. "Because you're an uncultured swine, you should read more."

"Is that any way to talk to your best friend?" He reaches for the book again. "Come on, what's the real reason?"

I pull open the hidden door beside him. "Because it's closed, it's soundproofed and this whiny little bastard won't shut the fuck up."

I walk through the door. The bound hooded figure in the steel chair immediately starts yelling through his gag. I slap him. "Shut the fuck up, we're not talking to you yet."

He pulls at the ropes holding him to the chair. Jerry frowns. "Who is he?"

"I made sure we took one alive from the hit on me."

"You collecting enemies now? Planning on opening a zoo?"

"I want to know who this crew are working for." I yank the hood from the man's head. Blood is pouring from the cut on his cheek, his eyes are swollen almost shut. Three teeth are missing.

I lean down close to him, lowering my voice. "Who hired you?"

"I've no idea. I just got a message offering me the job. Fifty thousand for one hit. If I'd known it was you, I'd never have taken it. Please, Don Caruso. Have mercy."

"You know my reputation. Have you heard of a time I showed mercy to my enemies?"

The man's eyes are wide with pure terror, his breaths coming out in ragged gasps. I give him a cold smile.

His eyes dart between us, searching for some semblance of pity. "Please," he says. "I don't know anything."

I sniff the air. "I can smell a liar." I nod toward Jerry who takes out his gun. "If the next words out of your mouth are anything but a name, your brains hit that wall behind you." The gun presses into his forehead. He winces as Jerry starts to squeeze the trigger.

"Vincent Marconi." He starts to blabber. "We were given the location, and the codes to the elevator control, but he never said it was you. Just said to take out whoever came out of the elevator…"

I silence him with a wave of my hand. Leaning down, I pat his sweat-covered hair. "That wasn't so tough was it?"

The man's face shifts from fear to a glimmer of hope. "So, you'll let me go?" he asks, his voice a blend of hope and desperation.

My smile is icy as I reply, "Of course not."

His face crumples in despair as he realizes the finality of his situation. "But I told you the truth! I confessed everything. Please, have mercy!" he begs, his voice now a pitiful wail.

"You took a contract involving my building, and you didn't think I'd have a problem with that? You saw that it was me coming out of the elevator and decided to try and kill me anyway. Now your crew's dead and you're going to join them. I hope it was worth it."

I signal to Jerry with a slight nod. "Make sure no one finds the body."

As Jerry moves in, the man's screams fill the room, a futile protest against the inevitable. "You're a monster, Dominic! A monster! You'll burn in hell for this."

I walk away, his screams fading into the background, the weight of his words leaving no mark on my conscience. I leave the store and look at the early morning sunshine. It's going to be a warm day.

Jerry appears next to me a minute later. "You think he's telling the truth?"

"I've no doubt."

"So Maria's brother is still alive. Who'd have guessed it?"

I look at him. "Find out what rock Marconi is hiding under and kick it over."

He nods. "You thought about how this might affect Isabella?"

"She's not a part of this."

"She came out of the elevator with you. They saw her face. Word gets back to him; she could become a hostage or worse."

He lights a cigarette and takes a drag. "I hate to say it," he continues, "but marrying her is the only way to keep her alive long enough for you to get over that obsession of yours."

I shake my head. "What the fuck are you talking about?"

"Word gets back to Marconi that she was with you. He puts two and two together and decides the best way to hurt you is to hurt her. Won't take him long to find out where she lives, will it?"

"He's no idea she means anything to me."

"You really want to take that risk? You've been watching her for six months. I know what she means to you."

I shake my head, my gaze fixed on the distant city lights. "I vowed to keep her away from my world, Jerry. She's twenty years younger than me and has her entire life ahead of her. And now you suggest I just put a ring on her finger?"

"Think about it. Under your protection, who would dare touch her? Fuck her a few more times, get this obsession out of your system. Kill Marconi, then get back to normal, stop all this stalking bullshit. It doesn't suit you."

I rub my chin, the weight of the decision heavy on me. "But dragging her into my world... She'll end up like me, desensitized to the violence, to the darkness. I can't do that to her."

"So, don't tell her about your world," Jerry suggests, his voice calm.

"I think she'd notice when I dragged her down the aisle."

"It's not going to take long to track Marconi down. Just tell her you need to stay married for a little while."

I glance at him, torn. "Remember what happened last time I got married?"

"So what are you going to do? Let him kill her?"

"Right now, Marconi has no idea what she means to me. I intend to keep it that way. For all he knows, she's an employee who got unlucky when she shared the elevator with me. I keep away from her, don't talk to her in public, don't do anything to draw attention to her. You find Marconi before he hires a more competent crew."

"If I didn't know you better, I'd say you wanted an excuse to keep watching her. You've fucked her once already, isn't that enough?"

I give him a look that I usually reserve for those about to die. "Nowhere near."

4

ISABELLA

Six weeks later...

I spot Sarah near the ice cream truck, her fiery red hair unmistakable even from a distance. She's got an easel set up and is hard at work painting the passing crowds.

"Isn't Bryant Park the most gorgeous place?" she asks as I reach her. "On the most gorgeous day too."

"You're in a good mood," I reply.

"Sold a painting yesterday." She sets her brush down, pointing to the picnic blanket beside her. "Care to join me?"

I sit beside her, doing my best not to bite my nails. She notices the tension at once.

"Not yet," I say before she gets a chance to ask.

"You don't know what I was going to say."

"You were going to ask me if I've taken the pregnancy test. It's in my handbag and I will do it, just not yet."

"Is the plan to leave it nine months and just see if anything pops out of your flaps?"

"Nice choice of word."

"Would you prefer cooter?"

"I'd prefer it if you let me decide when to take it." I lower my voice. "I'm scared. What if I'm pregnant?"

She takes my hand, her touch reassuring. "You need to know, Bella. Whether it's positive or not, it's better to face it. Come on, we'll do it together."

She folds away her art materials, tucking the easel under her arm as we head for the nearest public restroom. It's next to a long row of thick bushes and I can't help but feel eyes on me. I look into the undergrowth but I see nothing.

"What's up?" Sarah asks.

"Nothing. I'm just being paranoid." I head into the restroom and she follows me.

"Come on," she says, locking us into a stall together. "Let's find out if you're hitting that billionaire for child support."

"Is money all you think about?"

"Quit stalling in the stall. Piss on that stick, bestie."

I rummage through my handbag until I find the small, unassuming box. I draw it out, my hands visibly shaking.

She places a reassuring hand on my shoulder. "You've got this, Bella," she says, her voice a soothing balm to my frayed nerves.

I take a deep breath and open the box, extracting the pregnancy test. The plastic feels cold and alien in my trembling hands. I follow the instructions mechanically, as if on autopilot, my mind a whirlwind of what-ifs and maybes.

We wait in silence for the results. Sarah checks her watch, then looks at me, her eyes a mix of worry and support.

"How long has it been?" I whisper, not daring to look at the test.

"About five seconds," she replies softly. "Give it a chance."

The seconds stretch into an eternity, each tick of Sarah's watch amplifying the tension in the air. Finally, she nods at me, signaling that it's time.

With a hesitant hand, I reach for the test. My heart pounds in my ears as I brace myself for the truth. The display is clear, unequivocal: Positive.

A wave of emotions crashes over me—fear, confusion, a flicker of wonder. "It's positive, Sarah," I say, my voice barely audible.

She wraps an arm around me, her presence a comforting anchor in the storm of my thoughts. "Is that... is that good news?" she asks gently, her voice tinged with hope.

I shake my head, a whirlwind of emotions swirling inside me. "I don't know. It's complicated. He's so different from me. He's the type of guy who gets attacked in an office building for no apparent reason.

"I haven't seen him in there since. How do I get in touch with him? Ring the building and say I need to talk to the CEO, he got me pregnant?"

"Let's get some air," she suggests. "It smells of piss in here."

"I wonder why," I reply as she unlocks the stall.

We've barely stepped outside when a shadow detaches itself from the underbrush. A man in a tattered overcoat steps into our path, his intentions clear from the dangerous glint in his eyes.

"Hand over your purses, ladies," he growls, a blunt object glinting in his hand. "I'll shoot you both. Purses, now."

Before either of us can react, a blur of movement catches my peripheral vision. Dominic appears out of nowhere and in one fluid motion grabs the man's arm. He wrenches it backward with a strength that seems effortless.

"Drop the gun or I break your arm."

The mugger cries out, letting go of his weapon. "Please, you're snapping my fucking wrist. Fuck!"

I stare in shock as Dominic gets his hands around the man's throat, squeezing the life from him. "Stop," I shout. "You're killing him."

Dominic's eyes are burning like fires as he turns to look at me. "He threatened you."

"That doesn't mean you should murder him. Let him go."

"Run along," Dominic warns, loosening his grip. "Lucky for you, she's merciful." His voice is laced with a threat that sends a chill down my spine.

The mugger scrambles to his feet and takes off, stumbling in his haste to escape. Dominic watches him, ensuring he's truly gone, before turning his attention to us.

"Are you both okay?" he asks.

I nod, still in shock. "Yes, thanks to you. That was... incredible."

As he stands there, a calming yet enigmatic presence, I feel Sarah's curious gaze upon us. I take a moment to formalize introductions. "Dominic, this is my best friend, Sarah. Sarah, this is Dominic."

Sarah extends her hand, still slightly trembling from the encounter. "Where did you pop up from?"

Dominic's eyes briefly flicker, a subtle shift that doesn't escape me. "Just passing through," he replies with a casual shrug. He's clearly lying. Why?

Sarah nods, still eyeing him with a mix of gratitude and curiosity. "Well, we're lucky you were. It's not every day you have a guardian angel appear out of nowhere."

His gaze meets mine, and for a moment, I'm sure he knows that I see through the facade.

"Guardian angel might be a stretch," he says, a wry smile playing on his lips.

I can't help but smile back, despite the unease his mysterious appearance has stirred in me. "Well, you were our hero today, angel or not."

Sarah, picking up on the unspoken tension, quickly excuses herself with a knowing glance. "I'll see you later, Bella. You two have a lot to catch up on." She walks back to her painting spot, leaving me alone with Dominic.

He steps closer, reducing the entire world to just the two of us. "I've been thinking about you," he confesses, a hint of hunger flickering in his eyes. "Have you thought of me?"

His words catch me off guard, stirring a mix of emotions. "I... there's something I need to tell you," I stammer, struggling to maintain my composure.

He glances around him, like he's looking for something. "Not here."

"There's a good cafe around the corner. How about we get a coffee?"

"Sounds good." He looks around him again before giving me a smile that seems forced. "Let's move."

5

DOMINIC

We're supposed to be enjoying coffee on a rooftop terrace. My eyes keep darting to a suspicious glint on the roof opposite.

I tell myself it's just the sun hitting a skylight. It's been six weeks. If Marconi was going to take a shot at me, he'd have done it by now.

But I've kept away from her, just watched her in secret, until today. What if he's been watching her? Or me? Waiting to see if she means something to me?

She's sipping her coffee, looking even more beautiful close up. "How have you been?" she asks, her voice light, eyes curious.

Stalking you, I think to myself. Happy watching you from a distance, seeing that smile of yours when you talk to your friend, wanting those soft lips of yours wrapped around my cock more than anything else in the world.

I lean back, trying to appear relaxed. "Business has been busy," I say, keeping it vague. My world is no place for someone like her.

She doesn't need to know about the warehouse hit I missed last week because I was sitting outside her apartment in my car, waiting for her to come out.

Or the fact that my obsession has only grown stronger since we fucked. That it's taking every ounce of my self control not to bend her over this table and fuck her right here, in front of everyone.

Her gaze lingers on me, inquisitive and bright. "What kind of business are you in, exactly?"

I smirk, maintaining my facade. "I'm a businessman," I say, deliberately obtuse. "Dealing in various... ventures."

She laughs lightly, a sound that tugs at something deep inside me. "Like that ambush six weeks back? That kind of venture? Aren't you worried that might happen again?"

"Those men are dead now," I say, a hint of darkness seeping through.

Her laughter rings out again, assuming it's a joke. But I know better. The line between my reality and her perception of it is blurring dangerously.

"Seriously," she says. "What do you do?"

"You don't want to know. Trust me. Now, what did you want to tell me?"

She suddenly looks nervous. She sighs, leaning onto the table. Her elbow inadvertently nudges her cell phone, sending it clattering to the floor. She leans down, her hair cascading forward, to retrieve it.

The back of her chair explodes into splinters with a deafening crack, shards of wood flying through the air. Her eyes widen in shock, a gasp caught in her throat.

"Get down!" I shout, my voice laced with urgency. In a fluid motion, I lunge across the table, grabbing her. "Sniper."

We hit the ground together, a tangle of limbs and rapid breaths. I shield her with my body, my heart racing, every sense heightened.

The scent of her hair, the warmth of her skin beneath me—it's overwhelming, a dangerous cocktail of desire and fury. How dare anyone try to hurt her?

Another shot rings out, the bullet whizzing past us, embedding itself into the concrete with a thud. "Stay down!" I hiss, my mind racing as people scream and fight to get out of danger.

This is no random attack; it's a calculated strike. Aiming at her in order to hurt me. It's Marconi. I should have trusted my gut, got her out of here sooner.

He's been following me, waiting until I was with her to make his move. I was fucking dumb to think he wouldn't put the pieces of the jigsaw together.

I glance at Isabella, her face inches from mine. Her eyes, wide with terror, mirror the adrenaline surging through me.

"Stay close," I command, my voice a low growl as someone's hit, a body falling to the ground in front of me. I take hold of her cheeks, moving her so her eyes are fixed on me. "Focus. Don't raise your head. Follow me."

We move together, crawling across the terrace floor as more shots fire and more bodies fall.

We reach the exit, the cityscape sprawling below us. I reach up and open the door, ducking back down just as a shot hits the wood, sending splinters everywhere.

"Quick, this way!" I guide her down the stairs, taking them two at a time, my hand gripping hers firmly.

We burst onto the street level, a world away from the sniper's nest. Sirens are approaching in the distance but they'll be too late to help us.

I shove her into my car, a sleek machine built for moments like this. The engine roars to life. Tires screech against asphalt as we tear away from the scene, the city blurring past us.

Isabella's voice cuts through the chaos, her tone laced with fear and confusion. "What the hell is happening, Dominic?" Her eyes search mine, desperate for answers.

I glance at her, my mind racing with strategies and escape routes. "Someone's trying to kill you," I say, the gravity of the situation heavy in my voice.

"Me? Why me?"

"To hurt me."

My rear view mirror reveals a sinister black sedan weaving through traffic, its intent clear as it gains on us. "They're following us!" she cries out, her voice cracking under the strain.

"I can see that. Hold on."

I press the accelerator harder, the engine of my car roaring.

I navigate through the dense traffic of midtown Manhattan, each turn and swerve a calculated risk to lose our tail.

Sirens wail in the distance. I take a sharp left onto 42nd Street, narrowly missing a taxi while horns blare in protest.

"Who are they, Dominic?" Her voice trembles, her hands clutching the armrests. "Talk to me, please."

I glance at her, my jaw set. "It's complicated," I say as I weave between cars.

Another sharp turn, and we're speeding down Fifth Avenue.

I take a quick glance at her, seeing her face etched with anxiety and confusion. "I'll explain everything, I promise. Right now, I need to get us out of this."

I steer into a narrow alley between two buildings, barely wide enough for the car. The black sedan hesitates, losing precious seconds.

"We're going to get stuck," she yells, glancing behind her at the pursuing car. "They'll catch us."

"No, they fucking won't." I push the car to its limits, the sound of scraping metal hitting my ears. "Their car's wider than ours."

Ejecting out of the alley, we find ourselves on a quieter street in the Lower East Side. I check the mirror – the sedan is gone, for now.

She looks at me, her face a mix of relief and lingering fear. "I don't understand any of this. Who wants to kill me?"

I park the car in the shadow of an old, brick building, turning off the engine. The silence that follows is deafening. "It's my fault. There are people in my life who wouldn't think twice about using you to hurt me."

Her eyes search mine, looking for an anchor in the storm. "But why? What did you do?"

I reach for her hand, the contact a small comfort in a world turned upside down. "It's a long story. I'll tell you the whole thing later. But I swear, I'll do whatever it takes to keep you safe."

Before she can bombard me with any more questions, I pull out my phone, dialing Jerry.

"We had a sniper on us," I say when he answers, my voice low but tense. "Roof by Bryant's Park. You were right. Son of a bitch was waiting for me to meet up with her. And there was a car, a black sedan, tailing us." I give him the license plate.

His voice is sharp, urgent. "Got it. Any description of the sniper?"

I shake my head, even though he can't see me. "No, but it's got to be Marconi or one of his hires."

"Where's Isabella now? Tell me you didn't send her away again."

"I'm taking her to the safe house. And Jerry," I add, a decisive edge to my voice, "the wedding needs to happen."

Ending the call, I turn to face Isabella. She's staring at me, a mixture of shock and bewilderment in her gaze. "What was that about a wedding?" she asks, her voice barely above a whisper. "What wedding?"

I take a deep breath, my decision made. "We have to get married, Isabella. It's the only way to keep you alive."

Her reaction is instant and fierce. "Marry you? I hardly know you!" she exclaims.

"You'll only be safe as my wife," I explain, my voice firm.

"How does marrying you make me safe?" she demands, skepticism lacing her words.

"Because I'm not just a businessman. I'm a mafia boss. There are rules in the mafia. Marry me and you're protected by my name."

"That shooter didn't look like he was following the rules."

"He's an exception. His men wouldn't dare attack a Caruso family member."

"I don't believe you."

I glare at her. "I don't give a shit what you believe. We're getting married. That way you'll be safe from his hangers on while I deal with him."

Suddenly, my phone rings. It's Jerry again with news. "We found the car, occupants have been dealt with."

"Did they talk?"

"The sniper's Vincent. Wanted to take her out. Wedding is booked. That'll stop most of the trouble but how are you going to make sure he doesn't go after your blushing bride?"

"Honeymoon out of the country."

"Nice, perfect alibi while we whack Marconi."

"Precisely."

I hang up and turn back to Isabella, managing to resist smiling. "You're thinking about refusing," I say. "You can't. This is happening. You have no choice."

6

ISABELLA

I wake up in a luxurious penthouse. Modern art adorns the walls, sleek furniture sprawls across the room, and through the floor-to-ceiling windows, New York stretches out like a concrete jungle.

It's beautiful, yet I can't appreciate it. The moment I come to, I'm reliving the events of yesterday.

It was the same last night. Dominic dropped me off here and then left to do whatever mafia bosses do. All I could think of was how close I came to dying.

The shots, the other people falling, the blood. I couldn't even drink to block it out. In the end, I climbed into the guest bed and read one of Dominic's books until sleep finally overcame me.

My phone lies on the bedside table, a lifeline to the outside world. The battery died while we were running from the shooting. I get up and walk around the penthouse until I find a charger.

I plug it in, switch it on and dial Sarah. As soon as she answers, my words tumble out in a rush. "Sarah, it's me."

"Isabella? what's happened?" Sarah's voice is laced with concern. "I've been trying to call you. The shooting, were you anywhere near there?"

I take a deep breath, trying to steady my shaking hands. "They were aiming at me but they missed. Dominic saved me and brought me to his place. My phone died, I'm sorry."

"Are you all right? You want to meet up somewhere?"

"He says I can't leave. He's locked me in. Said it was for my own safety. He says we have to get married, and he's a mob boss."

Her sharp intake of breath is audible. "You need to call the police. This is serious! He's kidnapped you."

"He told me not to bother."

"And you listened? I know you had this stupid obsession with him but this is insane. Either you call the cops or I will."

"I'll call them now. I'm just still trying to make sense of everything."

"Ring me back when you've done it. Be quick." She hangs up.

I feel a knot of anxiety in my stomach. Dialing the police, I wait for an answer, rehearsing what I'm going to say.

"New York Police Department, how can I help you?" The voice on the other end is professional, detached.

Taking a deep breath, I muster the courage to speak. "Hi, I need help. I've been kidnapped."

The officer's tone shifts to one of concern. "Alright, ma'am, can you tell me your location? Are you in a safe place right now?"

I glance around the luxurious room, feeling a pang of irony. "I'm not sure. I'm in a penthouse. I don't know the address. It's in Manhattan somewhere, overlooking Central Park."

"Okay, ma'am, we're going to help you. Can you describe the person who took you? Do you know his name?"

My voice trembles as I answer, "His name is Dominic Caruso. He saved me from a shooting and then brought me here but all the doors are locked and I can't get out."

Suddenly, the officer's professional demeanor crumbles into fear. "Dominic Caruso? Miss, if this is some kind of test..."

"No, it's not a test!" I cut in, my desperation growing. "He's brought me to his penthouse, and I'm scared. I don't know what he wants from me."

There's a sharp intake of breath from the officer. "Miss, I... I can't help you. I wouldn't dare go against Don Caruso's wishes. Please, tell him I meant no disrespect by taking your call."

"But you're the police! You have to help me!" My voice cracks as I realize the extent of Dominic's influence. "Please, I'm trapped in here and I can't get out."

I suddenly become aware of a presence in the doorway. I turn, my heart skipping a beat, to find Dominic standing there with a wedding dress draped over one arm, his expression unreadable. It's clear he's been listening to the entire call. He strides over and takes the phone from my hand.

"Who is this?" he says down the line, pausing for a moment. "Adrian? How's your little boy? Good, I'm glad he's doing better. You take care now." He hangs up, passing the phone back to me. "I told you not to bother."

I recoil slightly, clutching the fabric of the chair for support. "I'm not marrying you," I state, trying to keep my voice steady as he holds the wedding dress out toward me.

Dominic's eyes lock onto mine, a predator assessing its prey. "I could force you," he says, his voice low and menacing. "You have five minutes to get changed. Get on with it."

7

DOMINIC

Standing outside the church in the rain, Isabella looks both ethereal and out of place in her wedding dress, the raindrops clinging to the delicate fabric.

She's stopped dead at the top of the steps, arms folded across her chest.

"Get inside," I tell her. "Vincent could be lining up a shot right now."

"I'm not going in there until you tell me the truth, Dominic," she asserts, her voice barely audible above the patter of the rain.

"What truth?"

"If we're getting married, we shouldn't have secrets, right? So why is Vincent Marconi trying to kill me? The truth or you'll have to drag me kicking and screaming down that aisle."

"He's the brother of my late wife, Maria. He wants revenge for her death."

Trapped by the Mafia Boss   39

Her reaction is immediate, her voice trembling. "Did you kill her?"

I fix my gaze on her, refusing to look away. "He believes I did."

"That's not what I asked."

"It was an arranged marriage. We were both young. It was a mistake. I never wished her any harm but I admit I felt nothing toward her. When she died, I was glad. Saved me a world of trouble."

My words hang in the rain-soaked air, a confession but not a full answer. "Vincent was in Sicily at the time. Got his head stoved in during a drug deal. I heard he was dead but it turned out he was in a coma for years. Woke up, and the first thing he did was hire a crew to kill me."

"At your building? When we got out of the elevator?"

"Exactly. When he saw us together today, he decided you meant something to me and decided to kill you to hurt me."

Isabella steps back, her expression one of terror. "God, you're going to kill me too aren't you. Oh, God, I'm going to die."

I grab her by the shoulders. "Think about it logically. Why would I marry you for your protection and then kill you? Sure, I've killed people but they deserved it. This is the only way to bring you under the Caruso family's protection, Then I deal with that psycho."

She looks up at the church, then back at me, her conflict evident. "And after we're married? What happens to me then? Lock me away somewhere? You're a murderer, Dominic, you said so yourself."

Before I can reply, Jerry emerges from the church, his black umbrella barely shielding him from the rain. "Boss, got some news."

"Go inside, Isabella," I say. She looks like she's about to argue. "Now," I add, making sure she sees the fury in my eyes. She looks terrified but it works.

She disappears inside. Jerry steps closer, his expression grave. "Marconi's planning to finish this today. I've got the jet ready to take you both to Portofino. You need to get the fuck out of here. Forget the wedding. Marry her in Italy if you have to. Just get moving."

His words resonate with me, cutting through the noise of my own pride. I glance at the church, thinking of Isabella inside, and my decision solidifies. "We get married first."

The thought of not being her husband is the only thing I fear at this moment. I have to have her as my bride, even if she's terrified of me.

I walk inside, leaving Jerry watch the exits with a team of lieutenants.

The interior of the church is a stark contrast to the gloomy weather outside. Stained glass windows cast colorful patterns on the stone floor, and the air is filled with the scent of old wood and incense.

A few witnesses watch in silence. They're being paid to be here but they've clearly heard the news. They all look like they're expecting the church to blow up at any moment.

I find Isabella standing at the altar, her wedding dress making her look like an angel in a place that feels too somber for her brightness. Her beauty is undeniable, but her eyes betray her apprehension, heightening my sense of guilt.

The priest shuffles out of a side room. A couple of guns appear before my men realize he's not a risk.

He's an elderly man with a white cane. His lack of sight seems to give him a different kind of vision, one that feels unnervingly perceptive. As he turns towards us. I swear he's looking into my soul. His brow wrinkles. He knows I'm a sinner. That much is clear.

"Dearly beloved, we are gathered here today..." his voice echoes through the church, solemn and resonant.

His words continue, his blindness somehow making the ceremony feel even more surreal. "If there is anyone who objects to this union, speak now or forever hold your peace."

"I object," Isabella says. "I'm here under duress."

"She's joking," I say, gripping her arm tightly. I lean over and whisper in her ear. "Do not do that again."

The silence that follows is heavy, filled with unspoken objections and the weight of our circumstances.

The priest coughs. "If I may continue. Do you, Dominic, take Isabella to be your lawfully wedded wife, to have and to hold, from this day forward, for better, for worse, for richer, for poorer, in sickness and in health, until death do you part?"

I glance at Isabella, her eyes meeting mine. There's a plea in them, a silent cry for a different life than the one I'm forcing her into. "I do," I say, my voice steady.

"And do you, Isabella, take Dominic to be your lawfully wedded husband, to have and to hold, from this day forward, for better, for worse, for richer, for poorer, in sickness and in health, until death do you part?"

Isabella pauses, a fragile breath escaping her lips. "Say it," I snarl at her.

"I do," she whispers, her voice laced with fear of me.

The moment hangs in the air, suspended and charged with a tension that feels almost tangible.

"You may kiss the bride," the priest declares, his voice echoing through the hallowed space. It's a command, a formality that seals this arrangement - not a union of love, but of necessity.

Yet, as I lean in, something deep within me stirs, a yearning that transcends the mere transaction of our forced marriage.

Our lips meet, hesitantly at first, like two cautious envoys unsure of the truths they bear. I feel her lips trembling, betraying her fear and apprehension.

Her body against mine is like marble, cold and unyielding. But beneath that, there's something else, a spark waiting to be ignited.

As the kiss deepens, I sense a shift. The walls she's built, the defenses she's raised, start to crumble under my touch.

Her resistance melts away, reluctantly surrendering to the undeniable pull between us. In our embrace, there's a silent confession – despite her fear, she's drawn to me, irresistibly so.

Her response awakens something fierce and almost animalistic within me. A dormant hunger roars to life, fueled by the intensity of her own desire mirroring mine.

Our tongues engage in a dance, a delicate tango of suppressed passion and denied longing.

We finally break apart, both gasping for air, and there's a new understanding between us.

"I hate you," she lies fiercely, her eyes burning into mine.

"I know," I reply, my voice low. "But your body tells a different story." I let my fingers trail teasingly along her arm, feeling her shiver under my touch. "I bet if I touched your pussy, it would be soaking wet."

"Stop it," she hisses, her voice a mix of desperation and desire. "Please, not here, not in front of everyone."

"Then you better behave, hadn't you, Mrs. Caruso?"

8

ISABELLA

Three weeks later…

I sit up in the large, plush bed, alone. The room, with its elegant furnishings and stunning view of the sea is no comfort after last night.

He didn't come to bed last night. Of course. To think I was worried about spending our nights together. I barely see him. I've spent my days working on my play, wondering if this is my life now.

I wrap myself in a silk robe and step out onto the balcony. Below me, Portofino is waking up; the quaint village with its colorful buildings and the serene sea should be a balm, but to me, it's a vivid reminder of my isolation.

My thoughts are a whirlwind - fear, resentment, and an unsettling confusion about my feelings towards Dominic.

The secret of my pregnancy weighs heavily on me. I turn around and notice a folded note on my bedside table. It's from Dominic. "Why not give Sarah a call?"

I frown. "Because you told me not to use my cellphone in case Vincent's tracking me," I say out loud.

My phone's on the floor, plugged in and charging. I'm guessing it must be safe. Maybe Vincent's already dead.

I call Sarah. As soon as she answers, my words rush out in a torrent of emotion. "Sarah, I feel so lost. Dominic, he's... I don't know what to think of him. One moment he's my savior, the next, I'm terrified he might be a monster."

Sarah's voice, filled with concern, is a lifeline. "Where are you?"

"Portofino. It's in Italy. We're staying in this villa that's been in his family for centuries. It's full of ghosts, I swear."

"You want me to call the cops?"

"I tried that. They're terrified of him. Look, he made me marry him."

"He did what?"

"This is technically our honeymoon. He said it's the only way to keep me safe from the man who's trying to kill me. But listen, I think he killed his first wife."

"What?"

"And I think I might be next."

My phone buzzes with an incoming message. I glance at the screen, a chill running down my spine as I read the ominous words: "I'll save you." An anonymous number.

I can hear the rumbling of Dominic's car engine coming up the drive. "I'll have to call you back."

I meet him in the entrance hall. His presence fills the room, a stark reminder of the power he holds over me. I only have to look at him to want to beg for sex. "Dominic, look at this," I say, showing him the message.

He takes my phone, his eyes narrowing as he reads the message. "Good," he says, a smile breaking out on his lips. "Took him long enough."

"Long enough to what?"

"Marconi's been tracking you via that thing. Now you've switched it on, he thinks he's got the upper hand but last night, I finalized my plans. I've got men watching all his haunts. As soon as he appears in public, he's dead." He kisses the top of my head. "I couldn't have done it without you."

"What are you talking about?"

"It had to be that way." He sees the anger in my eyes and his expression changes. "I needed you to tell Sarah you were scared of me. It had to sound genuine. This way, Vincent thinks I'll kill you like he thinks I killed my first wife. He wants to move fast, take you out before I do. So he pops up and we take him out."

"So you manipulated me? Why not ask me to tell her that?"

"Because it wouldn't have convinced him."

"I don't like being used like this."

"Won't happen again. He takes my hands in his. "I'm in love with you, Isabella. I will do whatever it takes to keep you safe. Listen, there's a festival in the square today. Give me a few minutes and we'll go together, all right?

"I know you've hated being cooped up but I had to make sure you were safe." He puts a hand on my shoulder. "I've been too busy arranging everything but that changes now. Thanks to you, Marconi will not see the sunset."

"I can't believe you faked a fight with me to make me call my friend and tell her I feared for my life."

"The machinations of the mafia boss. But don't worry, last time, I promise. From now on, nothing but honesty. Get dressed and we'll go and enjoy the sunshine. Anything you want to buy, it's on me."

∼

"I used to come every year when I was a kid," Dominic says as we walk through the crowded streets. "Haven't been back in years." He points up the top of a hill to a crumbling white stone building surrounded by smaller houses.

"That was the dance hall," he says with a wistful smile. "Was in there every weekend when I was a kid. It was where Maria's father proposed the marriage between us. Everyone heard. They all looked at me. How was I supposed to tell them she'd already slept with every guy in the town? Her father keeps talking about how pure she is and I'm standing there watching my father shake his hand and the deals made."

He pauses, like he's lost in the memory. "Vincent looked furious. He never liked me, thought his sister could do better. Told me I'd better take care of her. All the while she's looking around her like she's looking for an exit, eyes bulging, swallowing hard.

"Then she gets a hold of herself and acts like it's all great. She doubled the dose of her uppers the same day. By the time we were married, she was wired night and day, kept telling me she was going to kill me and take my money.

"Anyway, enough of that. It's in the past. Let's enjoy the festival."

We walk further into the village. Strings of lights crisscross above the cobblestone streets. The aroma of Italian cuisine — fresh pesto, grilled seafood, and sweet pastries — fills the air. A live band plays in the town square, their lively melodies inviting people to dance and celebrate.

"Do you see that gelato stand over there?" Dominic points to a small, colorful booth adorned with flowers. "When I was ten, I made a pact with my friends that we'd run it one summer, sell the best gelato in Italy."

His eyes sparkle with the memory. "We spent weeks planning flavors. I was obsessed with creating a perfect lemon gelato."

I can't help but smile, picturing a young Dominic with dreams of nothing more fancy than ice cream. "What happened?" I ask.

He sighs, the light in his eyes dimming slightly. "I was sent to the States to join my father, learn the family business. Everything changed. I never got to say goodbye to my friends."

The sudden shift in his demeanor tugs at my heart. The pain of such a sudden uprooting at a young age is palpable in his voice.

We continue walking, and he points to a cobblestone alley. "That's where I had my first kiss," he says with a half-smile. "Her name was Lucia. We were so clumsy and nervous. I think I bumped her head against the wall trying to be smooth."

We stop to watch a group of dancers performing a tarantella, their steps quick and precise. The music is infectious, a rhythm that seems to pulse through the crowd.

Before I realize what's happening, Dominic takes my hand and leads me into the dance.

At first, I'm hesitant, my movements stiff and uncertain. But as the dance progresses, I find myself being swept up in the energy, the music, the joy of the moment.

Dominic's hand is steady on my back, guiding me through the steps. Our eyes meet, and for a fleeting second, we're just two people lost in the rhythm, our troubles momentarily forgotten.

"Everything went wrong when I moved to America," he says as the song comes to an end. "I had to grow up pretty fast, saw my first dead man when I was twelve. My father wanted me to toughen up, get used to seeing corpses.

"He told me I'd be making some of my own soon enough. Passed me a gun and made me shoot this guy who'd tried to go to the cops. I remember standing there unable to pull the trigger until the guy laughed at me.

"Something snapped inside and I shot him. I never forgot the way my father patted my shoulder, told me he was proud of me. That I'd become a man."

As the music of the festival fades into the background, replaced by the gentle sounds of the night, Dominic and I walk back to the villa. The air between us feels different now, lighter somehow.

Emboldened by his openness, I find the courage to share pieces of my own history. "You know, my childhood wasn't exactly picturesque," I start, my voice soft under the starlit sky. "It's strange, but walking through the festival reminds me of moments I spent dreaming of a life like this."

Dominic looks at me. "Tell me about it."

"I don't talk to my parents anymore. They were... abusive, in more ways than one." The words taste bitter as they leave my lips, but there's a certain relief in voicing them.

"I used to dream the violence would stop, that we could move somewhere quiet and start again, forget everything that had happened. I used to think it was New York that made them like that but the truth is they'd have been the same wherever we ended up."

He stops, turning to face me, his concern evident. "I'm sorry you had to go through that."

I nod, feeling a tight knot in my throat. "I remember this one time, I'd won a school art competition. I was so excited to show them my sculpture. But when I did, my father just scoffed and smashed it up right in front of me. Said art would never put food on the table."

His hand reaches for mine, a silent gesture of support.

"And my mother," I continue, the memories flooding back now, "she was so cold. I used to make her breakfast in bed, trying to win her affection. She never ate it. Stared through me at the TV like I wasn't there."

The words start pouring out of me. "They used to hit me all the time. I was so scared. I didn't know what I was doing wrong. When I turned eighteen, I moved out, got a new cellphone, and I haven't spoken to them since."

As I speak, Dominic's expression hardens, the protective instinct in him awakening. "No one will ever hurt you like that again, Isabella. I promise you that."

"What if I'm like her?" I ask as we approach the villa. "What if I'm like that with my own kids?"

"You won't be."

"How can you be so sure?"

He kisses my forehead. "Because I know. Now lunch should be ready for us. Let's eat."

9

DOMINIC

The afternoon air is warm and fragrant, carrying the scent of the sea and blooming flowers. The sounds of the festival are faint from the villa dining room.

As we begin our meal, the soft clink of cutlery against fine china mingles with the distant lull of the sea.

I reach across the table, taking her hand gently. "Isabella, I know our beginning was anything but conventional. I want you to know, I deeply regret the way things happened.

"You shouldn't have been involved in any of this. When Vincent is dealt with, you'll be free to go get on with your life. I won't keep you trapped here with me."

"You think I feel trapped?"

"Don't you?"

My phone rings. "Caruso," I answer briskly.

"Dominic, it's Jerry. I have news." The voice is tense yet triumphant.

I stand up, moving slightly away from the table. "Go ahead."

"We found Marconi," Jerry says. "He was holed up in a safe house in Brooklyn. Came out just like you said he would. Had a bag packed. Looked like he was heading your way."

"Tell me he's dead."

"We made sure of it. Cut him into tiny little pieces."

"Good."

"You sound disappointed."

"Only that I didn't get to finish him myself. Any casualties on our side?"

"Two injured, but they'll make it. Marconi's men weren't expecting us. We had the element of surprise."

"Good work. Ensure the families of the injured are looked after."

"Already on it, boss."

Ending the call, I turn back to Isabella, my expression a mix of relief and contemplation. Her eyes are on me, filled with curiosity and concern.

"Is everything okay?" she asks, her voice soft in the night.

I take a deep breath, the weight of my next words heavy on my tongue. "Marconi is dead."

Her reaction is not what I expect. Instead of relief or indifference, she looks visibly saddened.

"I thought you'd be happy," I say.

"I am. It's just I'm scared."

"What are you afraid of? He's dead. He can't hurt you anymore."

"Dominic, I'm scared," she admits. "Scared of what this means, scared of losing myself in you."

I reach out to brush a strand of hair from her face, my touch gentle. "I'll always keep you safe, Isabella. I promise."

"But your last wife... I need to know what happened to her."

"It was a long time ago, it's ancient history."

"Clearly not to Marconi. What if there's anyone else out there wanting revenge for what you did?"

I shake my head. "He was her last surviving relative. We're safe."

"Look, I can admit I have feelings for you. Strong ones. But right now I'm being kept in the dark and I hate it. Please, you only need to tell me once but I need to know what happened."

I stare into her eyes and decide it's time to share my story. "We were driving to our honeymoon. She hated me. She never wanted to marry me but our parents arranged it. She started yelling about me ruining her life and that she was going to ruin mine and then it just happened."

"You shot her?"

"What? No. Of course not. Is that what you think of me?"

She's staring at me, eyes wide. "So what happened?"

"I should have noticed when she went for the parking brake but I was too angry to focus. She was telling me to stop and I was driving faster to try and shut her up and she just did it.

"She was crazy, grabbing the steering wheel and yelling that she'd rather be dead than married to a Caruso. The car spun out of control and hit a wall. When I came to, she was dead."

"But... I thought you killed her."

"I should have seen what she was going to do, should have stopped her. I might not have killed her but it was my fault she died."

She puts a hand on top of mine. "All these years, you've blamed yourself for her death? It wasn't your fault, Dominic."

She presses her lips to mine, our lips meeting in a tender yet passionate kiss. The kiss deepens, fueled by weeks of pent-up emotions and the day's revelations.

I gently pull away, my heart pounding in my chest. The weight of my dark past slowly lifts as her words wash over me like a cleansing rain. The dining room seems to fade away.

Her eyes sparkle with genuine affection, her touch soothing the wounds that have festered for far too long. I reach up and brush a strand of her hair behind her ear, my fingers lingering against her soft skin.

"Thank you, Isabella," I say.

She smiles, her lips curved in a way that could melt even the coldest of hearts. "You don't have to carry the weight of the world on your shoulders, Dominic. We all make mistakes."

Her hand finds mine once more, intertwining our fingers in a gesture of unity. "If anyone's to blame, it's your father. He forced you into a marriage."

"Like I forced you. I'm just like him."

"Are you? Because I see a man who would do anything to protect his wife."

Leaning in closer, I capture her lips once more, savoring the taste of her in every breath. Our kiss is filled with a desire that burns like a wildfire, consuming us both in its passionate embrace.

My hand slides slowly up her thigh, caressing the soft fabric of her dress. Heat emanates from her body, a reflection of the fire raging within me.

With gentle yet deliberate movements, I lift the hem of her dress, revealing the tantalizing glimpse of her bare skin. Her breath hitches as anticipation fills the air.

Lowering myself to my knees, I trail kisses along her inner thighs, relishing in the delicate taste of her skin. Her body quivers beneath my touch, responding to every stroke and caress.

Slipping her panties down her legs, they pool around her ankles, leaving her completely exposed. I look up at her, my eyes meeting hers in a glance that speaks volumes.

I lower my mouth to her pussy, savoring the taste of her, the warmth of her, the very essence of her.

Her body shudders beneath me, her moans filling the room as she approaches the point of no return.

I feel her climax building within her, the tension rising like a tempest, threatening to pull us both into its vortex.

As she screams out my name, her body convulsing in desire, I continue to explore her, to give her pleasure, to show her just how much I want her.

In the midst of her orgasm, I feel a surge of my own desire, an overwhelming need to possess her completely. I pull her dress off her body, revealing her perfect form beneath.

Her skin is warm and smooth.

As she continues to shudder with pleasure, I reach for myself, pulling my cock from my pants. I stroke it gently, imagining her lips around it, her tongue swirling around the head, the warmth of her mouth enveloping me.

I move to sit on her chest, pushing my cock straight into her mouth.

She eagerly takes me in, her lips wrapped around my shaft, her tongue teasing the sensitive head. The sensation of her warmth and wetness enveloping me is beyond words, it's pure ecstasy.

She sucks and strokes me, her hands deftly moving in rhythm with her mouth, building my pleasure to a fever pitch.

As I begin to thrust in and out, I lean down to whisper in her ear. "That's it, take it all in." She moans around my cock, her body language expressing her own desire and satisfaction.

I continue to fuck her mouth, my pace increasing with each thrust. I watch as her eyes flutter with pleasure, her face wet with saliva and my precum.

The room is filled with the sounds of our passion - her soft moans and my heavy breathing mingling with the wet slurping noises from her mouth.

But I can't wait any longer. I have to fuck her.

I pull out of her mouth. As I position myself at her entrance, I look into her eyes. I want to spend the rest of my life staring into those eyes.

With one powerful thrust, I enter her, feeling her warm walls surround me like a vice. Her breath hitches, and she lets out a muffled cry, her body arching up to meet mine. My hips piston, our bodies moving in perfect harmony.

She moans with pleasure as my thrusts become harder and more intense. Each stroke brings with it a new wave of pleasure, and she tightens around me.

"Yes," she whimpers, her voice hoarse with desire. "Fuck me, fuck me harder."

I obey, thrusting even deeper into her, my cock pounding against her most sensitive spots. I watch as her body tenses, her face contorting into a mask of pure ecstasy. Her eyes roll back, and her cry is a symphony of lust and release.

As her orgasm washes over her, I move harder and faster, feeling my own climax building.

With a final, powerful thrust, I release within her, my cum filling her up, as she shakes with pleasure, her body spasming around me.

As we come back down to earth, I pull out of her, and we collapse onto the dining room floor, our bodies sticky with sweat and cum.

"I have to tell you something," she says as she sits up, her voice filled with tension all of a sudden. "You've been honest with me and I haven't."

"What is it?"

"I'm pregnant."

10

ISABELLA

"How long have you known?" Dominic's voice cuts through the quiet, a mix of hurt and accusation.

I hesitate, the weight of his gaze heavy upon me. "A few weeks," I admit, my voice barely above a whisper. The fear of his reaction, the uncertainty of our future, it all culminates in this moment.

His expression darkens, the lines of his face hardening. "A few weeks? And you chose to tell me now?" There's a dangerous edge to his tone, one that I've come to associate with his power, his control.

I can't help but recoil slightly, the fear that has been simmering inside me starting to boil over. "I was scared. Terrified of what this means, of what you might do.

"Your world is not like mine. It's filled with danger and violence. And I thought you killed your wife. I didn't know what you were capable of."

His gaze never wavers.

"I found out the day we were at the park," I confess, the memory vivid in my mind. "I took a test in the restroom. I was about to tell you when..."

My voice trails off, haunted by the memory of the sniper's bullet that shattered the peace of that day.

"When you almost got shot."

"Since then, I've been too scared. But I can't keep secrets from you, not like this. It's too important. Please tell me you're not angry."

He nods slowly, processing my words. "Is it from... that time in the elevator?"

"Pregnant from my first time," I say, a small smile touching my lips despite the gravity of our conversation. "I'm like one of those girls you read about in the magazines. Condom not working, teen mother, right?"

Dominic's expression softens, a mix of wonder and apprehension. "I never thought... I mean, with my age. I'm not a young man anymore, Isabella."

I reach out, touching his face. "And I thought I was too young for you. That you wanted me only for physical reasons." My voice is a whisper, laden with past insecurities.

He shakes his head, his eyes burning with intensity. "Isabella, you've given me something I didn't dare hope for. You're teaching me how to live again, to see beyond my empire. You sure you want a baby with me? I'll be pushing sixty when they head off to college."

"And you'll still be the man I love. Promise you're not angry."

"I understand why you kept it to yourself. I don't agree but I understand. I'm not the most approachable of men but that can change. I can change. If you're happy, I'm happy."

"I am happy now it's out in the open."

"Tell me something."

"What?"

"Have you ever been sailing? I think we should get out on the water."

～

As Dominic and I board his sailboat docked in the bay, the clear azure sky reflects the calmness blossoming in my heart.

The gentle breeze and rhythmic sound of waves against the hull wrap around us, creating an almost ethereal ambiance.

"Nervous?" he asks as I wrap a life vest around myself.

I shake my head, feeling a mix of excitement and nervousness. "A bit, this is a first for me."

"There's nothing quite like being out on the open sea."

I watch him expertly handling the boat as we drift further from shore. I feel my apprehension melt away, replaced by awe.

Standing at the bow, my hair dancing in the wind, I gaze out at the vast expanse of water.

I catch Dominic watching me, his eyes reflecting a mixture of admiration and something deeper.

"Isn't it beautiful?" I ask, turning to him with a genuine smile.

"It is," he replies. "Never seen an ass as sweet as yours."

We drop anchor in a secluded cove, surrounded by water that glimmers like sapphires. At Dominic's suggestion, we dive into the cool embrace of the sea.

The mood shifts as we find ourselves alone on the beach, enveloped by nothing but sea and sky. Dominic reaches for me, pulling me close.

Our kiss starts gently, but soon deepens with a passion that speaks of our deepening connection.

His fingers trace patterns on my back, sending shivers down my spine.

"I love you," he whispers, his breath warm against my ear.

"I love you too," I reply, my voice barely above a whisper.

Dominic's fingers find mine, intertwining them together as we gaze out at the sea. The sun is starting to set, casting a warm glow over everything.

The sky is painted with hues of orange and pink, the colors reflecting on the water.

"This is perfect," I say, leaning my head on Dominic's shoulder.

He nods in agreement, his free hand coming up to stroke my hair. "It really is," he says softly. "Just the two of us, away from the world, in this little slice of paradise."

As if sensing my thoughts, Dominic leans in closer and presses a gentle kiss to my forehead.

"You know," he begins, his voice filled with tenderness, "I never imagined I could find such peace and happiness in another person until I met you."

"You've brought so much light into my life," I say softly, my voice filled with sincerity. "I can't imagine my days without you by my side."

His eyes lock with mine, his gaze intense yet filled with love. "And I can't imagine spending my days without you either," he replies, his voice carrying a hint of vulnerability.

"You complete me in ways I never expected. You are my everything." He kisses my cheek softly.

"I want to make you feel cherished," he adds, his voice husky with desire. "To show you just how much you mean to me."

A wicked smile tugs at his lips as he reaches for my swimming costume, deftly removing it with his skilled fingers. The fabric falls away from my body, revealing my skin beneath, glistening in the fading light of the afternoon.

"You are so beautiful," he murmurs, his eyes locked on mine as he traces the curve of my breast with his fingertips.

My heart races as anticipation builds between us, the tension growing thicker with each passing moment.

His lips graze my skin, his breath warm and inviting. He takes his time, exploring every inch of my body with tenderness and care.

I arch my back, pressing into his touch, my body begging for more.

His hands roam over my body, his fingers sliding under the lace of my underwear, stroking me gently.

I moan into his mouth, my desire for him growing stronger with each passing second.

He slowly, delicately, traces the contours of my body with his tongue, leaving a trail of fire in his wake. Each touch, each kiss, building on the last, until I'm ready to beg for more.

Finally, his lips reach their destination, and I gasp at the sensation. His tongue is warm and wet, exploring my most private places with care and precision.

I arch my back, moaning softly, as his tongue caresses me, sending delicious waves of pleasure coursing through my body.

My nerves are on fire, every touch sending an explosion of delight from head to toe. I'm lost in this moment, wholly consumed by the sensation of his lips and his tongue.

I don't know how long we're down there, but time seems to stand still as he works his magic. Each stroke is more intense than the last, and I find myself overwhelmed with desire.

I need more, I want more, and he gives it to me, never once breaking eye contact.

"I'm close," I whisper, my voice shaking with need. "Please, Dominic. Don't stop."

He smiles, a devilish glint in his eyes, and continues his attention, his mouth moving from my most private spots to my most sensitive ones, drawing out my pleasure with a gentle, steady rhythm.

Each stroke is more intense than the last, and I find myself lost in a haze of desire and ecstasy.

I cry out his name, my body trembling as the orgasm hits me like a tidal wave. It washes over me, consuming me completely, and I feel like I'm floating on air, weightless and eternal.

Dominic doesn't stop, continuing to stroke and caress me as I ride out the aftershocks of my climax.

I'm still tingling from my orgasm, my body sated yet alive with desire.

"Ready to swim back?" he asks.

I look at him with dazed eyes. "I don't know what my own name is. Give me a minute."

He smiles. "I can give you all the time in the world. You're my wife."

11

ISABELLA

The morning in Portofino is bright and clear as Dominic and I drive to the local clinic.

I can't help but smile. We spent last night in bed together as husband and wife.

I woke up this morning next to him and I felt safe and secure. It's a feeling that lingers.

As we walk into the clinic, Dominic's phone rings. He answers with his usual calm demeanor, but within seconds, his tone shifts drastically.

I watch him, his jaw clenching. "What do you mean he's still out there?" he snaps into the phone, his voice laced with barely contained fury.

"I want every resource we have on this. Find him!" He ends the call abruptly, slamming his fist into the nearest wall

The sudden display of anger sends a shiver down my spine. It's a stark reminder of the life Dominic leads, a life filled with danger and violence. A life I'm about to bring a child into.

"Is everything okay?" I ask tentatively.

Dominic exhales sharply, trying to compose himself. "It's Marconi. The man we thought was him? It was a body double. He's still a threat. He could be coming for us right now."

The news hits me like a ton of bricks. Marconi, the shadow looming over our lives, is still out there. And here we are, about to bring a baby into this world of uncertainty. "Should we go back to the villa?" I ask.

He shakes his head. "This appointment is important. We'll go back as soon as it's done."

We are greeted by an elderly doctor, Dr. Bianchi, who has a gentle, grandfatherly demeanor. His eyes light up when he sees Dominic.

Behind the warmth I see anxiety, tension. Is this the reaction Dominic inspires? Fear? Has his reputation preceded him even here?

"Ah, Dominic! Last time I saw you in this clinic, you were no bigger than a grape in your mother's belly," Dr. Bianchi exclaims, a nostalgic smile on his face.

Dominic manages a strained smile, but his agitation is palpable. "It's been a long time, Doctor," he replies curtly.

Dr. Bianchi, seemingly oblivious to Dominic's mood, ushers us into the examination room. "And who is this lovely lady?" he asks, turning his attention to me.

"This is Isabella," Dominic introduces me, his voice softening slightly.

"Congratulations to you both," Dr. Bianchi says as he begins the ultrasound. "Let's see how your little one is doing."

As the doctor starts the check-up, the image of our baby appears on the screen, and for a moment, all the tension in the room dissipates. I can't help but feel a surge of emotion at the sight.

"There you go," Dr. Bianchi says, pointing at the screen with a twinkle in his eye. "A healthy, growing baby. About ten weeks, I'd say. You can see the jawbone there already, and the upper lip. There's the heart, you see that?"

Dominic, despite his earlier anger, looks at the screen with a mixture of awe and tenderness. "That's our baby," he whispers, more to himself than to anyone else.

"The organs all look like they're in the right place. You've nothing to worry about."

Dominic's phone rings and he curses under his breath. "I'll be right back," he says, walking out of the room.

The moment he's gone, Dr. Bianchi's expression changes. "I'm sorry," he says, bursting into tears. "He said he'd kill my grandchildren."

"Who did?" I ask as a side door opens. "Dominic?"

I find myself looking into the eyes of the man I rejected at the screenwriting workshop. Vincent Marconi.

"Hello, Isabella," Vincent says, pointing a gun at me. "Alone at last. Don't scream or I kill the doctor. Walk this way, no sudden movements if you please."

I walk over to him, staring at the gun barrel until he grabs my arm, dragging me out of a back door and into a black car.

He keeps the gun trained on me. "Dominic thinks he's so clever," he sneers as he starts the engine. "While his men wasted time watching my double, I made my way here. Now it's time for us to go somewhere more private before we call your husband. Pass me your cellphone."

I do as he asks and he slows for long enough to dump it out the window. "Don't want him tracking us down before we're ready, do we?" he asks. "Now we can be alone for a while."

His words send chills down my spine. "Why are you doing this?" I manage to ask, my voice trembling.

He looks at me with hatred. "Because Dominic murdered my sister."

I look out the window and see the derelict mansion Dominic showed me during our tour of the village.

We pull into the garage. Marconi's grip on my arm is tight and unyielding as he drags me out of the car and into the building.

12

DOMINIC

"Come on, Isabella, pick up," I mutter under my breath, a mixture of frustration and fear beginning to set in. I call a third time, my grip tightening around the phone.

Still no answer. The unsettling silence on the other end of the line sends a chill down my spine.

Dr. Bianchi is looking at me in terror from the far side of the room, muttering apologies. "If she's dead, so are you," I tell him, loading the tracker on my phone.

"Please," he replies. "I had no choice."

"You better pray she's alive. Don't even think about running. I'll find you."

I sprint outside, climbing into my car, my mind racing with possibilities, each more unsettling than the last. Vincent's killed her. He's torturing her right now. He's loading her into a plane.

It's all my fault. I shouldn't have brought her into this. The tracker pings. Half a mile from here. She's not far away.

The drive is tense, each passing second stretching out forever. As I pull up at the tracker's location, the sinking feeling in my gut intensifies. A cellphone in the middle of the road.

I pick up the phone, turning it over in my hands. It's then that it rings, jarring the silence around me. My blood runs cold as I answer the call, my voice a mix of rage and desperation.

"Where's my wife?" I demand, the words a growl of barely restrained fury.

The line crackles, and Marconi's voice slithers through. "You'll never find her, Dominic. I'm going to have such fun with her. You can listen if you like."

"Tell me where she is, Marconi!" I demand, my voice laced with fury and desperation. "Or you'll die screaming."

"I'm going to kill her when I'm done but not for a... hey, what are you doing? Come back here."

There's a sudden commotion on the other end of the line. I hear shouting, the sound of a scuffle, and then, unmistakably, gunshots.

"The old dance hall," I hear Isabella yelling before the phone call ends abruptly, leaving me in a deafening silence.

I know where she is. I just need to get there in time.

The old dance hall looms ominously before me; its once-grand architecture is now a decaying shell. I park the car just out of sight, making my way on foot.

Fresh tire tracks mark the ground outside, and there's a car in the garage, hood still hot. They're here for sure.

Stepping inside the mansion, the heavy air of the past envelops me. The eerie silence is only broken by the distant flap of pigeon wings in the rafters.

The musty smell of decay fills my nostrils — old wood, peeling wallpaper, a history of neglect. The mansion's grandeur is long gone, replaced by a haunting desolation.

I move methodically, my footsteps muffled by the thick layer of dust that carpets the floor. I see other prints and I follow them.

Faded paintings hang crooked on the walls, furniture is draped in ghostly sheets, and chandeliers loom overhead, their crystals dull with years of dust.

The prints lead to a door at the end of a narrow, cobwebbed hallway. It's locked, the wood swollen and warped with time.

I press my ear against it, listening for any sign of movement inside. My heart thunders in my chest as I prepare myself for what lies beyond.

With one swift, powerful kick, the door gives way, splintering under the force. I raise my gun, every muscle tensed, ready to confront whatever — or whoever — awaits me.

Inside, I find Isabella, her eyes wide with fear, standing in a corner. The relief that floods through me is indescribable. "Isabella!" I exclaim, rushing to her side. "Did he hurt you?"

"It's a trap," she yells, trying to push me away. "Behind you!"

"Well, well, well. Isn't this touching?" I spin around in time to find Marconi, gun trained on Isabella. "You shoot me, she dies. Drop the gun."

The air in the decrepit mansion is thick with tension as I face off with Marconi. His gun is trained on me, a twisted satisfaction in his eyes. "Now," he snaps.

"Why don't you drop yours and we'll decide this like men."

"Play it that way. Say goodbye to your wife."

But I'm not about to let him take Isabella from me. I've faced too much, lost too much to let it end here. He goes to pull the trigger. I shove her to the side, firing my gun as I move.

My bullet grazes Marconi's arm, causing him to stagger back, his own shot missing us both, embedding itself in the decaying wall behind us.

"Isabella, run!" I shout.

But she doesn't run. Instead, she grabs a heavy candlestick from the mantelpiece beside her. With a fierce cry, she tosses it at Marconi, catching him off guard as he fires wildly.

The candlestick crashes down on his gun hand, forcing him to drop his weapon. I scramble to my feet, rushing to Isabella's side. Together, we stand, a united front against Marconi.

He looks at us, his eyes filled with rage and disbelief. "You think you've won?" he spits, blood dripping from his wounded arm. "I'll take you both down with me!"

"Killing me won't bring Maria back."

He laughs, a harsh, grating sound. "You're a killer, just like me. Don't cloak it in nobility. Does she know how many people you've murdered in your time?"

His eyes, wild with fury, are fixed on the gun lying haphazardly on the floor. He lunges for it, cursing me as he does so.

My body moves before my mind fully catches up, driven by a survival instinct as old as time. I jump forward, intercepting his path.

I grab his arm, my fingers locking around his wrist with an iron grip, I twist it backward in a swift, calculated motion. His face contorts with pain, his rage now mixed with the sharp sting of physical agony.

"Control, Marconi," I hiss, my voice a cold blade cutting through the heated air. "That's what you lack. All the rage, none of the control."

I wrench the gun from his weakened grasp, my actions precise and unforgiving.

In a fluid turn, I pivot, the gun now firmly in my control. His eyes widen, the realization of his predicament dawning upon him. The tables have turned. "Let's talk about this," he says, an ingratiating smile on his lips. "What do you say?"

"I say you threatened my wife." I pull the trigger. Then again, a second shot to make sure he's dead.

As the echo of the gunfire fades, a heavy silence descends. His body goes limp, and I let it fall to the floor.

Isabella approaches me. Her eyes are wide, but not with fear. "That's why I'm not afraid of you. That's why I know you'll be a good father. You can control your anger."

She clings to me, her body trembling from the ordeal. "I thought I'd never see you again. I ran and he shot at me. I remembered you said this was the dance hall. I shouted but I didn't know if you heard me."

"That's why you'll make a good mother," I say, holding her tightly, the realization of how close I came to losing her sinking in. "The ability to think on your feet. Come on, let's get out of here."

13

ISABELLA

Sitting in the dimly lit living room of the villa, the weight of the day's events hangs heavily between us.

Dominic stops his restless pacing and comes to sit by me, his expression a turbulent mix of emotions.

He takes my hands in his, his grip firm yet filled with an underlying tremor of emotion. "Isabella, I've put you through so much," he begins, his voice rough with self-reproach.

"This world I live in, it's not for someone like you. I dragged you into this mess, and for that, I'm deeply sorry. The thought of losing you today... it's unbearable. If you wish to divorce when we get back to the States, I'll understand."

I search his eyes, seeing the raw honesty and the pain of his admission. "It wasn't your fault. You've done everything you could to protect me," I say, trying to offer him some comfort. "And yes, it was terrifying, but I choose to be with you."

There's a knock at the door. Dominic's body tenses.

"Stay here," he instructs, a protective edge to his voice.

"No chance," I reply, following him out into the hall. "I'm safer with you."

I watch as he opens the door, ready to confront whatever or whoever might be on the other side. My heart pounds in my chest, the fear of the unknown momentarily gripping me.

But then I see his body relax slightly, a sign that there's no immediate danger.

As I approach, I see the local police officers standing at the door, their expressions serious but not threatening.

I hover in the background, watching the exchange unfold with bated breath. The officers, their faces somber, exchange a brief glance before addressing Dominic.

"Mr. Caruso, we're aware of the situation regarding Vincent Marconi," one officer begins in English. "And while we must follow the law, we also remember the support your family has provided to this village over the years."

Dominic nods, his expression unreadable. "I understand your position. The Caruso family has always valued our relationship with the local community."

The first officer nods. "In light of this history, we've decided to deal with Vincent's situation discreetly, out of respect for your family. But we advise caution.

"The less attention drawn to this matter, the better for all parties involved. We recommend you return to America while the body is dealt with."

"Thank you, officers," Dominic says sincerely. "Your understanding in this matter is greatly appreciated. The Caruso family will not forget this."

As the officers depart, the tension in the air dissipates. Dominic turns to me, his eyes reflecting a mix of relief and concern.

"Well, that's one less thing to worry about," he says, trying to offer a reassuring smile. "Now what about the doctor? Do you think I should kill him?"

"I think we should find a new doctor, back in New York. This one apparently didn't get the memo on pregnant women needing to avoid stress."

14

DOMINIC

I gaze out at the vast expanse of ocean below the jet window. In my hand a glass of rich red wine. Isabella sips on mineral water.

The calm after the storm of recent events feels surreal, almost dreamlike.

"So, have you thought about any baby names?" I ask, turning towards her.

She smiles, her eyes sparkling with the thought. "I've always liked the name Sophia for a girl. It's classic and elegant."

I nod, swirling the wine in my glass. "Sophia is beautiful. And for a boy? I was thinking maybe Pietro. Strong, traditional."

She laughs, a sound that fills the cabin with warmth. "Pietro and Sophia, they sound like characters from a Shakespeare play."

"That reminds me, how's the play you're writing?"

She sighs, looking down at her hands. "I've been procrastinating too much. You gave me an excuse with all the shootings and forced marriages but I don't know if I'll ever get it finished."

I lean in, my tone firm but supportive. "When we get back, I'll help you set some goals. Make sure you have the time and space to focus on your writing. Spank you if you don't meet your deadlines."

Her eyes meet mine, filled with lust. "That won't encourage me to work harder! But what about your work?"

"What about it?"

"I'm presuming you need to get back to it. How can you spare the time to watch over me?"

"I'll make sure to delegate as much as I can," I assure her. "I don't want to miss a moment of this parenting journey with you. I'll be there every step of the way."

She reaches out, her hand finding mine. "About that spanking?"

I smile at her, the corners of my mouth lifting in response to her playful inquiry. Her eyes sparkle with anticipation, a mix of mischief and desire dancing within them.

I watch her closely, captivated by her graceful movements, as she takes deliberate steps towards me.

With a gentle gesture, I guide her to the plush leather seat in front of her. The supple material embraces her form as she bends over it in a position that made her vulnerable.

I lift her dress and pull her panties down slowly, tracing lines down her soft skin. I allow my hand to caress the curve of her backside.

I gently tease her, my fingers dancing closer and closer to her ass. Finally, after what feels like an eternity, my palm slaps down, the sound echoing around the cabin.

Her eyes widen in surprise, but there is a flush of excitement in her cheeks that can't be ignored. The corners of her mouth curve into a smile as I spank her again, this time with a little more force.

Her moan is music to my ears as she leans into the sensations, inviting me to continue.

I bring down my hand time and time again, each strike eliciting a gasp or cry of pleasure from her lips. The soft leather of the seat muffles her cries, as if it were absorbing every ounce of her arousal.

As I spank her, I begin to rub her ass, soothing the sting of my hand on her skin. Her body trembles beneath me, every muscle tense with anticipation and desire.

"Do you like it, sweetheart?" I whisper in her ear, my breath hot against her skin. "Do you want more?"

Her breath hitches as she nods. "Please. It feels so good."

I increase the intensity of my strikes, each one landing with a sharp crack against her flesh. She cries out in a mix of pain and pleasure, her body arching towards me as if seeking more.

And so it continues, the rhythmic slap of skin against skin, punctuated by her moans and gasps.

I move my free hand down her body, tracing the curve of her hip and the crease where her thighs meet her pelvis.

As she squirms beneath me, I dip a finger into her wetness. She groans loudly, her body arching further as I slide it inside her.

Her muscles clench around me instinctively, coaxing me to delve deeper.

I began to finger her, my movements meeting the rhythm of the spanking I continue to give her.

As my fingers worked their magic on her, I push one of them ever so slightly into her rear entrance.

Surprisingly, she doesn't protest; instead, she pushes back against me, silently giving her permission to invade that forbidden territory.

With a bit more pressure, I'm able to slide in a finger, feeling the tightness of her ass clench around my intrusion.

A shiver runs through her body as I pump my fingers in and out of both holes, hitting her sweet spots with each thrust.

"You're so wet," I murmur, my voice low and filled with arousal.

She lets out a small whimper as I press against her clit, her hips bucking under my touch.

"That's it," I growl. "Come for me, baby. Let me see you come."

I increase the pace of my fingers, thrusting in and out of her with a fervor that matches her own. Her moans grow louder, her body tensed as she reaches the precipice of orgasm.

"Yes!" she cries out, her voice hoarse with passion. "I'm going to come!"

Her body shakes violently, her muscles clenching around my fingers as she climaxes.

As her orgasm subsides, I slowly pull out of her, feeling the wetness of her desire on my fingers.

I move my fingers to her face, smearing her arousal across her cheeks, her lips, and her chin. She opens her eyes, a look of surprise and pleasure on her face as she realizes what I was doing.

"You're so beautiful," I whispered, my voice filled with awe.

Her breath hitches as I step out of my pants, revealing my erection waiting to be claimed.

With a tender smile, I guide myself inside her, our bodies connecting in a way that is both intimate and electrifying.

She moans softly as I slowly move within her, my hips moving in a rhythm that matches the beat of our hearts.

Her muscles clasp around me, her body taking in every inch of me as if it is the only thing that can bring her pleasure. Her moans grow louder, her body trembling with each thrust.

"That's it," I say, my voice filled with awe. "Take all of me."

Her breasts bounce softly, a sight that makes my cock throb with desire. Her moans grow louder and more intense, and her muscles clench around me, her body trembling with each wave of pleasure.

"Come for me, baby," I pant, my voice low and rough. "Let me feel you come around me."

She cries out, her body arching up to meet mine as she reaches the pinnacle of her pleasure.

I thrust into her one last time, feeling my own orgasm building. It hits a moment later and I pull out, splashing onto her thighs and stomach while staring up at her.

"You're marked as mine now," I tell her. "For the rest of your life."

"Wouldn't want it any other way."

"I want to marry you. Properly this time. A wedding that you've always dreamed of, with our families and friends, a celebration of our love and the life we're building together. Will you marry me?"

"Can I wipe your cum off me first?"

"If you want a traditional wedding, I suppose you should."

15

ISABELLA

One week later...

As I sit waiting for Sarah to arrive at the park, my hand instinctively goes to the ring that Dominic has given me.

It's more than just a piece of jewelry; it symbolizes a new chapter, a commitment renewed under the promise of a better future.

I think of the rooftop terrace, the sniper, the danger, all gone forever. I feel safe, especially knowing Dominic is probably out there somewhere, watching me.

When she arrives, her eyes are immediately drawn to the ring on my finger. "Isabella! That's gorgeous!" she exclaims, her face lighting up with joy.

I can't help but smile, feeling a surge of happiness. "We're going to have a proper wedding this time, with everything we missed out on the first time. You'll be maid of honor, right?"

"Of course. When did you get back?"

"I'm sorry, I know I should have called but I've been so busy."

So, spill the details! When's the big day?"

"We're thinking of a spring wedding. It's our favorite season, and it gives us enough time to plan everything."

"Spring is perfect! Romantic and beautiful," Sarah gushes. "What about the venue? Somewhere local, or are you thinking destination?"

"We're considering Portofino, where he's from," I reveal, my heart fluttering at the thought. "He's given me an unlimited budget to make it happen. Fancy a vacation paid for by my husband to be?"

Sarah's eyes widen. "A wedding in Italy will be so romantic. And the dress? You have to have the perfect dress!"

"I've been looking at designs by Elie Saab," I say, picturing the elegant gowns. "Something classic and elegant, with intricate lace detailing. I want it to be timeless, ageless, like him."

"What about the food?"

"We want a mix of traditional Italian cuisine and some international dishes. Fresh seafood, handmade pasta, and of course, a spectacular wedding cake," I describe, my mouth watering at the thought. "Thought you might like to provide a painting of the happy couple?"

"It's like something out of a movie. You and Dominic are going to have the most beautiful day."

I nod, feeling a wave of happiness wash over me. "It's more than I ever dreamed of. And having my best friend there will make it even more special."

She squeezes my hand. "I wouldn't miss it for the world. This is your fairytale, and I can't wait to see it all come together."

Sarah's eyes gleam with genuine interest as we shift topics. "I almost forgot. What about the play?" she asks, stirring her coffee. "How's that coming along?"

I take a deep breath, feeling a wave of pride. "It's almost finished," I say. "Been working almost nonstop since I got back. I've been inspired. I told myself I couldn't speak to you until it was done. That's what pushed me through."

"That's great." She leans in closer, her curiosity evident. "You never told me how Dominic took it when he found out about the pregnancy. I'm assuming that part went okay?"

A soft smile spreads across my face at the memory. "Actually, he was wonderful about it. I was so nervous, scared of how he would react, especially with everything going on in his life. But when I told him, he was just... perfect."

Sarah's eyes sparkle. "Perfect? Do elaborate!"

"He was surprised, of course, but then he was incredibly supportive," I explain. "He reassured me, promised to be there every step of the way. I just wish I'd told him sooner."

"Told you!" She reaches across the table, giving my hand a gentle squeeze. "That's because you found someone who truly loves you for who you are, and that's rare."

"He's been my rock through all of this. And he's already so protective of the baby. He talks to my belly every night before we sleep."

Sarah chuckles. "That's so sweet. He's going to be a great father."

I nod, feeling a sense of contentment. "I think so too. He's more than I ever hoped for in a partner."

"But it's time for more important talk."

"What about?"

"Deciding which band is going to play at your wedding."

16

DOMINIC

Seven months later...

Isabella is lost in the throes of labor. I'm at her side, holding her hand, feeling a profound sense of awe and helplessness.

It's a stark contrast to the control and power I'm accustomed to in my world. I can do nothing to ease her pain and it's killing me.

Sarah is also in the room, ready with snacks and words of encouragement.

Her presence adds a layer of warmth and familiarity, easing the tension slightly. The few times I was busy during the pregnancy, Sarah was there for her friend.

The labor room is a whirlwind of activity, the tension palpable in the air. Isabella, with her face etched in pain and determination, grips my hand tightly.

"Isabella, you're doing amazing," I tell her, my voice attempting to sound calm and reassuring, though inside, I'm a tumult of concern and helplessness. "If killing a doctor would take the pain away, I'd do it in a heartbeat."

The medics give each other anxious looks as Isabella manages a weak smile. "So romantic. Maybe some more pain relief would do the trick."

"Pain relief, now!" I roar to the medics who scurry around me as Isabella takes my hand.

"Calm down or you'll get thrown out."

"They wouldn't dare."

"They might not but I will. I don't want doctors scared for their lives working on me. Cool it." She gives me a weak smile and my love for her grows even stronger.

As the hours drag on, her labor intensifies, her pain becoming more pronounced. Sarah, ever the supportive friend, is by her side, offering water and words of encouragement.

Her presence is a comfort, yet I can't shake off the feeling of helplessness.

Watching Isabella in such distress, a protective instinct, fierce and raw, surges within me.

I turn towards the doctors, my voice laced with a menacing edge. "Do something about the pain. She's suffering too much. You have to make it stop."

Isabella, through her exhaustion and pain, looks at me with a mixture of love and exasperation. "They're doing everything they can."

As the tension in the labor room reaches its peak, I stand by Isabella's side, feeling a tumultuous mix of emotions. Her grip on my hand is both fierce and reassuring, a lifeline between us as she endures the final stages of labor.

"You're nearly there, Isabella. Just a few more pushes," the doctor encourages, her voice calm and steady.

Isabella, with beads of sweat on her brow and a look of sheer determination in her eyes, nods weakly. "You can do this," I say, kissing her brow.

Sarah, standing on the other side, wipes Isabella's forehead with a cool cloth. "You're the strongest person I know, Isabella. You've got this."

With each contraction, her breathing becomes more labored, her efforts more intense. The room is filled with a sense of urgency, the medical team ready and waiting.

"Alright, Isabella, big push now," the doctor instructs, her tone both encouraging and commanding.

With a deep breath and a cry of effort, Isabella pushes with all her might. I hold my breath. The room falls into a brief, tense silence, followed by the most beautiful sound – our baby's first cry.

The doctor quickly and efficiently clears the baby's airways. "Congratulations, it's a boy," she announces, her face breaking into a smile.

As she hands me our son, wrapped in a soft blanket, my hands tremble with a mixture of joy and awe. "He's here, Isabella. Our son, Pietro."

Isabella, exhausted yet radiant, reaches out to cradle our baby. As she holds him close, a look of pure love and wonder washes over her face.

"Hello, my little one," she whispers, tears of joy streaming down her face. "You had me worried for a while there. Thought you'd never come out."

I lean in, placing a gentle kiss on Isabella's forehead and then on the soft, downy head of our son. "You're both my everything," I say, my voice thick with emotion.

As I cradle him for the first time, a wave of indescribable emotions washes over me. He's so small, so fragile, yet his presence fills the room with an immense power.

I'm awestruck by the immediate bond I feel with him, a connection that's both primal and profound.

"Isabella, look at our son," I say, my voice choked with emotion. I carefully hand our baby to her, watching as she gazes at him with a mix of wonder, love, and sheer relief.

"He's perfect," she whispers, tears of joy rolling down her cheeks. "We did it, Dominic."

I lean in, kissing her forehead gently. "You did it, Isabella. You're incredible. I love you both so much."

"We love you too, don't we little guy?"

Sarah steps closer, her eyes misty with emotion. "Congratulations, you two. You're going to be amazing parents. Now, I get to become the godmother, right?"

17

ISABELLA

Six months later...

As I walk down the aisle, enveloped in the soft rustle of my elegant gown, the guests turn their heads, their faces alight with anticipation. Sarah smiles, Pietro asleep in her arms.

The grandeur of the church, with its stained glass windows casting colorful patterns on the floor, adds to the solemnity of the moment.

My heart beats with a mixture of excitement and nerves, but as my eyes find Dominic at the altar, a sense of calm washes over me.

He stands there, the epitome of elegance in his perfectly tailored suit, his gaze filled with love and a quiet strength that reassures me.

Reaching the altar, I take his hand, feeling the warmth and certainty of his grip. The priest, with his kindly eyes and an easy smile, steps forward to begin the ceremony.

"Friends, family, we are gathered here today to witness the reunion of two people whose hearts have found a home in each other," the priest begins, his voice resonating in the hallowed space.

"I've known the Caruso family for many years, and I've had the pleasure of watching Dominic grow into the man he is today."

He glances at Dominic, a twinkle in his eye. "I remember a young Dominic, always the adventurous spirit, climbing the highest trees, much to his mother's dismay.

"But even then, he had a sense of responsibility, a care for those he loved. It's that heart which has led him to Isabella, a remarkable woman whose strength and grace are evident to all."

The guests chuckle softly, and I squeeze Dominic's hand, sharing a private smile.

"Love," the priest continues, "is not just a feeling, it's an action. It's a choice to stand by each other, through the climbs and the falls of life.

"Dominic and Isabella have chosen to renew their vows together, to support, respect, and cherish each other."

He looks out at the congregation, his expression serene. "I've seen how they look at each other. It's a look that speaks of deep understanding, of a bond that goes beyond words. In their eyes, you see not just love, but a friendship, a partnership."

The priest's words resonate with me, echoing the depth of what Dominic and I share. As he leads us through our vows, the significance of each word, each promise, fills my heart.

"I now pronounce you husband and wife," he declares, his voice warm with joy. "You may kiss the bride."

As Dominic leans in, his kiss is a seal of our love, a promise of a lifetime together. The guests erupt in applause, their happiness surrounding us like a warm embrace.

We move the event to the grand ballroom of the villa, alive with the sounds of music and laughter.

Guests, a blend of Dominic's relatives and influential associates, mingle with Sarah and me, creating a harmonious blend of our two worlds.

The room is beautifully decorated, the tables adorned with elegant floral arrangements, and the soft glow of candlelight adds a touch of romance to the atmosphere.

Sarah approaches us with a beaming smile. "Pietro's happy with his nanny, playing with his teddies. You two look absolutely stunning," she exclaims.

"Thank you, Sarah," I reply, feeling a surge of affection for her. "It means so much to have you here with us."

Dominic nods in agreement. "Your support has been invaluable. We're both grateful for it."

She gives us a playful wink. "Well, I wouldn't have missed it for the world. Now, go enjoy your party! And I expect to see some serious moves on the dance floor."

The moment for our first dance arrives. The band begins to play a soft, romantic melody, and Dominic leads me to the dance floor.

As we embrace and start to move to the music, the rest of the world seems to fade away.

"You look beautiful tonight, Isabella," Dominic whispers, his eyes locked on mine.

I smile, resting my head against his shoulder. "This feels like a dream. I never thought I could be this happy."

He pulls me closer, his voice low and full of emotion. "Every day with you is a dream. You've brought so much light into my life. I promise to make you this happy every day, for the rest of our lives."

The sweetness of his words fills my heart with warmth and love. Around us, our guests watch, some with tears in their eyes, touched by the depth of our connection.

As the song ends and we draw apart, the room applauds. We share a lingering kiss, a seal on our promises and dreams.

The rest of the night is a blur of happiness, a celebration of our love and the journey we've embarked upon together.

∼

As we step onto the villa balcony late into the night, the scent of the sea mixed with the fragrance of blooming flowers from the gardens below fills the air.

Dominic wraps his arms around me from behind, his lips brushing against my neck. "I can't think of a better place to start our new life together, my wife" he whispers, his voice filled with emotion.

I turn to face him, my heart full. "Me neither. This is perfect, my husband."

The moon shines down upon us, casting a soft glow on our faces. His touch sends shivers of anticipation down my spine, his fingertips tracing delicate patterns along the curve of my back.

Slowly, he unravels the fabric that drapes my body, revealing the secrets hidden beneath layers of satin and lace.

His eyes meet mine, filled with a reverence that takes my breath away.

The absence of panties is a secret I've kept, one that makes him growl with lust as his fingers find where they should have been.

Gently, Dominic's hands find their way to places untouched by anyone but him. With each caress, he weaves a tapestry of pleasure that leaves me breathless.

I surrender myself to his touch, basking in the sweet ache that builds within me.

A gasp escapes my lips as his finger grazes the forbidden territory of my ass, a place of vulnerability and raw pleasure.

The intensity of the sensation sends shivers coursing through my body, amplifying the connection between us.

My husband knows me like no other. He understands my cravings, my hunger for exploration and intimacy.

With gentle insistence, he delves deeper, coaxing waves of ecstasy to crash against the shores of my being.

I whisper in his ear, my voice filled with both need and tenderness. "I want to feel you inside me, Dominic. I want us to have another baby."

His fingers move with a new urgency, setting a rhythm that matches the pounding of my heart.

The anticipation grows, building toward a crescendo that threatens to consume us both.

He pauses for a moment, his breath ragged, and gazes into my eyes.

"Are you ready?" he asks, his voice hoarse with desire.

I nod, my breath caught in my throat. He positions himself inside me, and with a deep, slow thrust, he enters me completely.

My body responds in kind, wrapping itself around him, pulling him closer with each undulation of my hips. I move so I'm riding him, grinding down on the base of his cock.

"I'm close," he whispers, his voice strained. "I want to feel you come with me, to make you pregnant again."

I smile, the words sending a surge of electricity through my body. "Let's make a child together."

With a final burst of energy, I ride him hard, urging him toward the release we both seek. Our bodies, bathed in sweat and desire, pulse in unison, our breaths mingling in the sultry air.

"Come for me," I plead, my voice filled with raw emotions and hunger.

And with those words, he surrenders to the tide of pleasure that has been building within him. I feel his seed spill into me, the warm, life-giving essence of him filling me completely.

The sensation tips me over the edge and I cry out with pleasure, my body shaking as my climax races through me.

"I love you," he whispers, his breath warm against my skin.

"I love you too," I reply, my voice trembling with emotion. "So glad that elevator got stuck. I might still be working on my play right now, instead of married to you with a baby and hopefully another one on the way."

He kisses me softly. "Fate brought us together, nothing on earth can keep us apart."

18

DOMINIC

Five years later...

Tonight marks another milestone in our journey together. We're at the opening night of Isabella's new play, "Shadows to Light."

The excitement in the air is palpable as we take our seats, the auditorium filled with an eager audience.

As the lights dim and the curtain rises, I feel Isabella's hand gently squeeze mine.

This play, her latest creation, is a reflection of her life's journey, a narrative of overcoming darkness to find strength and happiness.

The stage comes alive as soon as the curtains go up. The protagonist battles her past demons to forge a path of resilience and hope, mirroring Isabella's own experiences.

With each play she's written, she's brought out more of her own life story. The audience is captivated, of course. They hang on every word and every emotion portrayed on stage.

When the final scene concludes, the theater erupts into a standing ovation.

The applause is thunderous. I turn to look at her, her eyes shining with a mixture of pride and joy.

"You did it again, Isabella," I whisper, my voice filled with admiration. "Your story, it's touched so many."

She smiles, a look of contentment on her face. "It's our journey, Dominic. From shadows to light. And this is just the beginning."

"You mean there'll be a sequel?"

"Maybe child number three?"

The rest of the evening is a blur of congratulations and celebrations. Friends, family, and admirers approach us, praising Isabella's work.

As the crowd starts to thin and we prepare to leave, Isabella turns to me, her expression earnest. "None of this would have been possible without your love and support, Dominic. You gave me the strength to turn my experiences into something meaningful."

She lowers her voice. "And you spanking me every time I got distracted was a big help."

∽

It's a bright, sunny afternoon, a few days after enjoying the success of Isabella's play. Our New York home is filled with the sound of laughter and the innocent chatter of our four-year-old child and our two year old.

Two lively and curious souls with a penchant for exploring every nook and cranny of our spacious garden. Pietro and Sophia. The reason my heart is so light despite the darkness of my work.

As I sit on the garden bench, watching them play, I'm struck by the profound transformation in my life.

Pietro, at four years old, is a bundle of energy, chasing after butterflies with a curiosity that knows no bounds.

Sophia, two years younger, sits nearby, meticulously arranging pebbles into patterns, her focus and attention to detail mirroring my own.

The days of navigating the murky waters of the mafia feel like a lifetime ago. Now, my world revolves around legitimate business ventures and providing a safe, prosperous future for my family.

Isabella joins me, her eyes following our children with a mixture of love and amusement.

"What do you think they'll be when they grow up?" I ask.

"Pietro is going to be an explorer, I think," she says, a smile playing on her lips. "And Sophia, well, she might just be an artist or an architect with that focus of hers."

I can't help but laugh. "He certainly has your sense of adventure, and she seems to have inherited my penchant for detail."

Isabella's expression turns more serious. "Dominic, the changes you've made, leaving so much of your past behind for a legitimate life... it means the world to me, to all of us."

I nod, my gaze drifting back to Pietro and Sophia. "It's the only way. I want them to grow up in a world where they don't have to worry, where they can chase butterflies or arrange pebbles without a care."

As if on cue, Pietro runs over, a dandelion in his hand and a bright smile on his face. "Look, Daddy, Mommy! I found a magic flower!" His voice is filled with excitement and wonder.

"I make castle," Sophia chimes in, holding up a small arrangement of stones she's put together.

I take the dandelion from Pietro and admire Sophia's stone castle. "You both are amazing," I say, and they beam with pride.

The evening unwinds in a flurry of laughter and family warmth. We play board games on the living room floor, Pietro's competitive streak emerging as he tries to outsmart us.

Sophia, with her gentle nature, seems more interested in the colors and shapes of the game pieces.

Later, we settle into cozy armchairs, reading their favorite stories, their little faces alight with wonder and excitement at each turn of the page.

These simple, unadorned moments with Isabella, Pietro, and Sophia are what I cherish most.

It's these quiet evenings, filled with the innocent laughter of our children, that signify the profound change in my world.

As bedtime approaches, we start the nightly routine. First, I tuck Pietro into his bed, his room adorned with posters of space and dinosaurs, reflecting his ever-growing curiosity about the world.

"Goodnight," I say, ruffling his hair affectionately.

"Night, Daddy! Can we go to the park tomorrow?" he asks, his eyes already heavy with sleep.

"We'll see," I reply with a smile, turning off the light and leaving the door slightly ajar.

Then, Isabella and I move to Sophia's room, a soft, pastel-hued space. As we tuck her in, she reaches up, wrapping her small arms around our necks. "Love you," she murmurs, her voice drowsy.

"We love you too, sweetheart, more than anything in the world," I respond together, my heart swelling with a love so deep and protective it's almost overwhelming.

After planting a gentle kiss on her forehead, we watch her eyelids flutter closed, the soft rhythm of her breathing a soothing melody in the quiet room.

As we step out, closing her door softly behind us, Isabella and I share a look of contentment and gratitude.

Back in the living room, Isabella and I settle on the couch, a comfortable silence enveloping us. I take her hand, feeling a profound sense of gratitude.

"Isabella, these five years have been the best of my life. You, Pietro, and Sophia, you're my world," I say, my voice thick with emotion.

Isabella leans her head on my shoulder, a contented sigh escaping her lips. "Dominic, I feel the same. We've created something beautiful together. It's more than I ever dreamed of."

She nestles closer, her head finding its place on my shoulder as if it were a custom-made groove meant only for her. A tender smile graces her lips, radiating warmth that fills my heart with joy.

The crackling fire casts a mesmerizing display of flickering shadows across the room, creating an enchanting dance of light and dark.

I lean in closer to her ear, my voice laced with playful affection. "You know," I whisper softly, "your next play... it seems you're falling behind on the word count."

"I haven't started writing it yet." She turns to me, her eyes gleaming mischievously beneath thick lashes.

A smirk tugs at the corner of her lips. "Oh? Falling behind? Yes, I am," she replies, her voice tinged with a teasing undertone. "Sorry, Sir."

"Well," I respond, my voice filled with mock seriousness, "we can't have that, can we? It seems some disciplinary action may be necessary."

With a swift motion, I guide her to stand before me. The flickering fire casts an ethereal glow on her skin, accentuating the curves of her body.

As she stands there, her clothes clinging to her form, I can't help but admire the way desire dances in her eyes.

I take a step closer, my hands gently tracing the contours of Isabella's face. She leans into my touch, a soft sigh escaping her lips.

I slip my fingers beneath the hem of her shirt, slowly lifting it up and over her head. It falls to the floor in a soft whisper, leaving her bare before me.

My gaze roams over her exposed skin, taking in the beauty of each curve and contour.

With a flick of my wrist, I undo the clasp of her bra, allowing it to fall away and reveal her firm breasts.

My mouth finds her nipple, teasing it with tender kisses and gentle bites that elicit a soft gasp from Isabella.

Her hands weave through my hair, pulling me closer as if seeking more.

I oblige, my lips traveling down her body, tracing a path over her stomach and hips before settling on the waistband of her pants.

I tug them down, exposing her legs and the lacy underwear that matches her bra. She steps out of them, kicking them aside as she stands before me in nothing but her lingerie.

My fingers trace the delicate lace, teasing the sensitive skin beneath.

With one swift movement, I tear away the last barrier between us, leaving her completely naked.

I guide her to the couch, my hands gentle and reassuring as I help her lie down.

Her body lies before me. I can't resist the urge to explore her further, to touch and taste every inch of her skin.

I kiss her softly, our lips meeting in a fusion of desire and love.

My hands move down her body, tracing the curve of her hip and the gentle slope of her waist.I part her legs, my fingers brushing against the sensitive skin of her inner thighs.

As I lower my mouth to her pussy, she trembles beneath me.

Her breasts rise and fall with each ragged breath she takes, her body straining towards mine as if she can't resist the desire that courses through her.

I taste the sweet nectar of her desires, my tongue exploring the intimate folds. Then, I suddenly flip her over and spank her ass.

The sound of her flesh slapping against my hand echoes through the room, a reminder of the passion that burns within us.

She moans softly, pushing back against me, her body inviting me in. I slide a finger inside her, our bodies melding together as if they were made for this moment alone.

As desire takes over, the rhythm begins to quicken. I can't wait any longer. I position myself behind her, my cock now poised at her entrance. I take a deep breath and plunge inside her.

Her breath hitches, her body arching back against mine as I begin to fuck her from behind. The sound of our bodies coming together fills the room.

I bring her to the brink of orgasm before sliding out, lubing her ass with one finger, slapping her buttocks with my other hand.

She lets out a gasp, her body tensing up as I begin to push my cock into her ass.

My hands grip her hips, guiding her movements as we begin to find a rhythm.

I pull back and thrust forward, my hips slapping against her ass. The sound reverberates through the room, the only sound in the otherwise quiet house.

She moans softly, her body trembling beneath me.

The intensity builds, the sweat dripping down our bodies, our skin slick against each other. She moans out my name, her voice hoarse with passion.

Her ass clenches around me, the sensation sending waves of pleasure coursing through me.

I can't hold back any longer. My hips thrust harder, my body trembling in tune with hers. I thrust deeper, my balls slapping against her ass.

As I reach my climax, I feel myself too deep inside her ass to pull out. Instead, I hold her close, my cock pulsating within her, our bodies shaking with the force of the orgasm.

We lie still for a moment, our hearts pounding, our breaths coming in ragged gasps. Then, we turn towards each other, our bodies glistening with sweat and desire.

She traces her fingers along my face, her eyes filled with love and passion.

"That was... beyond words," she whispers, her voice husky with desire. "How does it keep on getting better?"

"Because it's with the right person," I reply. "My perfect wife."

YOU MAY ALSO LIKE

Married to the Mafia King is my first full length forced marriage mafia romance. It's now available on Amazon and here's a sneak preview of chapter one for you to enjoy…

PREVIEW - MARRIED TO THE MAFIA KING

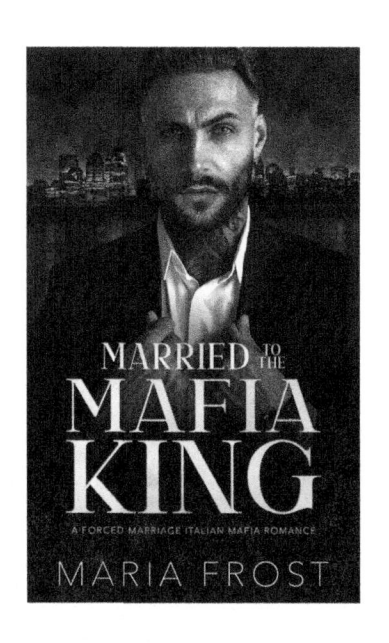

BLURB

I owe him money. He's making me pay whether I want to or not.

An obsessive mafia boss just broke into my house.

Shoved me straight down to my knees.

But the most dangerous man in New York isn't here to kill me.

He's here to claim my V-card all for himself.

Because my father made a secret deal with the mob.

Sold every inch of my trembling curves to this Italian devil.

He's possessive, controlling, and fifteen years older than me.

And now he's ravaging me over and over.

Telling me I will marry him.

I will submit.

Whether I want to or not.

CHAPTER ONE

I shove the door open, stopping dead at the sight that greets me.

Clothes spread across the floor, drawers pulled out, cupboards hanging open. Has it finally happened? Have dad's debts finally caught up with him? It sure looks like it.

A shuffle of movement catches my eye. I turn to find my neighbor, Mrs. Henderson, peering in at me.

"Never did get the damp sorted, did he?" she says, her nose wrinkling. "I told him when he moved in here that he needed to get it fixed, what with your mom having a baby on the way and all.

"What are you now, twenty-one? And the place still stinks. I said to Reggie, God bless his soul, those new neighbors of ours are moving in, and the pipes are shot, and she's seven months gone and-"

"Do you know where my dad is?" I interrupt. "Did he talk to you at all?"

She shakes her head. "Ran out of here with a suitcase in one hand and a wad of cash in the other. He asked if he could borrow some money and I said I could maybe lend him ten.

"He laughed at me and said he needed fifty thousand or some mafia boss was going to have him killed. He begged me to help. I said I didn't have that kind of money and he just got in his car and raced off."

She sighs. "And those tires of his need looking at. Bald as my Reggie, God bless his soul."

"Gone," I say to myself. "So many times he threatened to run out on me. I never thought he'd actually do it."

She reaches past me, picking up a photo of my mom. "She was a good lady, your mother. Too good for a man like him."

She sets the photo down on a shelf. "You'll be better off with him gone, trust me. I hear him yelling at you through the walls. Thin as paper they are. You're like your Mom. You put up with too much bullshit from that asshole, excuse my French."

I manage a weak smile. "You remember much about my mom?"

"She had beautiful eyes, like yours. Never said a word in anger, that woman. Working on those books of hers day and night to the end. When she wasn't traveling on those research trips. Worked so hard, unlike your father. She's with the angels now though, her and my Reggie, looking down on both of us."

She glances out through the window. "Rain's coming. I better go get the sheets in. Only just put them out." She squeezes my shoulder lightly. "You let me know if you need anything, won't you?"

I give her a nod and watch her leave, my eyes moving slowly back to the photo of my mother. She passed when I was a year old, leaving me in the care of a father who was always more interested in drink than parenting.

I move through to the kitchen, looking for any clue as to where my father has gone. His name is on the mortgage. If he's gone for good, I haven't just lost my job and the last of my family today. I'll be homeless too.

The table is buried under a mishmash of unpaid bills, crumpled fast-food wrappers, and torn up betting slips. A note is pinned to one of the cupboards with a rusty steak knife. The handwriting is jagged and menacing.

Today, or we burn it down with you and your kid inside.

I've barely finished absorbing the grim message when the back door bursts open. My heart catapults into my throat as three men walk in, one after another.

The first man, a towering figure, cracks his knuckles menacingly. Beside him, a leaner figure with a cold, calculating expression, surveys me with a gaze that feels like ice. The third lazily twirls a bat in one hand, a smirk playing on his lips.

The leader, eyes as hard as flint, locks his gaze onto mine. "Your father owes the Garibaldi family fifty thousand dollars," he growls, his voice a rough scrape against the silence of the room. "Where is he?"

Panic grips me, my heart thundering in my chest as I shake my head, words tumbling out in a desperate rush. "He's gone. I don't have any money. Please, you have to believe me."

His laughter mocks me, filling the cramped space and twisting the knife of fear even deeper. "Sure was low of your old man, leaving a pretty thing like you behind to face the music."

He leans closer, the stench of tobacco wafting off him. "Let me paint you a picture, sweetheart, since you seem to be in the dark. Your dear daddy was more than just a drunk. He was a gambler too. Took a big loan from my boss." He laughs. "Now, the mafia don't like it when debts go unpaid. Payment's due and we're not leaving here without it."

The room spins as his words sink in. My father borrowed money from the mob?

He chuckles at my disbelief, the sound devoid of any warmth. "See, we're not unreasonable," he continues, his voice venomous. "We simply want what's ours. Fifty grand. And seeing as your father is nowhere to be found, you're going to help us recover that loss, one way or another."

The man with the bat steps forward, his smirk widening. "With looks like yours, you could easily earn that kind of money. Ever been touched, sweetheart? You hiding a pretty virgin pussy under there? Want to show us?"

As he reaches for the hem of my skirt, a surge of adrenaline prompts me to slap his hand away. His response is swift; a backhand across my face that sends me reeling. My cheek stings, the taste of iron filling my mouth.

"Your dad knew we were coming," he sneers into my ear, his breath hot and foul. "Abandoned you, knowing what we do to girls like you. How does that make you feel about daddy dear?"

The leader, his hand inches from violating me, is suddenly airborne, yanked back by an unseen force. I look behind him. A giant of a man is tossing him aside as if he's nothing but a rag doll.

The newcomer is wearing a jet black suit, his eyes burning with fury. "You killed him," one of the other men says in disbelief.

I look down at a corpse, the neck bent at an impossible angle. "Touch her and you die," my savior growls, turning his attention to the other two men.

Apologies spill out, a desperate attempt to save themselves from the wrath of my unexpected hero as they set off running.

In their haste to flee past me, they stumble over their own feet, one barely making it out but the other is too slow. The stranger has him by the throat, lifting him effortlessly off the ground.

The thug kicks his legs, his hands clawing at the stranger's arm, trying to pry away the vice-like grip cutting off his air. "Help," he wheezes, turning his gaze to me. "He's killing me."

My hero only releases his grip when the thug's chokes have faded into a wet gurgle. He lets go at last and a second body joins the first on the floor.

The room spins as I try to make sense of the chaos, my gaze flitting between the unmoving figures on the floor and the enormous brute striding toward me.

My knees hit the ground with a soft thud. "Please," I beg, my voice a desperate whisper. "Don't kill me. I'm sorry, okay. I'll find the money. Just please don't hurt me."

"I'm not here for money," he replies, fixing me with a stony stare that makes me shudder.

"Then what are you here for?"

"You."

~

READ THE COMPLETE STORY HERE

ALSO BY MARIA FROST

The Forced Marriage Mafia Bosses

1 Taken by the Mafia Boss

2 Trapped by the Mafia Boss

3 Auctioned to the Mafia Boss

4 In Debt to the Mafia

∼

The Rossi Mafia Brides

1 Married to the Mafia King

2 Married to the Mafia Devil (coming soon)

Married to the Mafia Boss

(Exclusive to mailing list subscribers)

Printed in Great Britain
by Amazon